THE FROG LAKE MASSACRE

Bill Gallaher

VICTORIA · VANCOUVER · CALGARY

TouchWood Editions
108 – 17665 66A Avenue
Surrey, BC V3S 2A7
www.touchwoodeditions.com

TouchWood Editions
PO Box 468
Custer, WA
98240-0468

Library and Archives Canada Cataloguing in Publication
Gallaher, Bill   The Frog Lake massacre / Bill Gallaher.

ISBN 978-1-894898-75-1

    1. Frog Lake Massacre, Frog Lake, Alta., 1885--Fiction. 2. Cree Indians--Alberta--History--19th century--Fiction. I. Title.
PS8563.A424F76 2008   C813'.6   C2008-903108-3

Library of Congress Control Number: 2008905353

Proofread by Sarah Weber
Cover design by Chyla Cardinal
Cover image: Glenbow Archives, NA-4118-2

Printed in Canada

TouchWood Editions acknowledges the financial support for its publishing program from the Government of Canada through the Book Publishing Industry Development Program (BPIDP), Canada Council for the Arts, and the province of British Columbia through the British Columbia Arts Council and the Book Publishing Tax Credit.

This book has been produced on 100% post-consumer recycled paper, processed chlorine free and printed with vegetable-based dyes.

For Jaye—again and always

CONTENTS

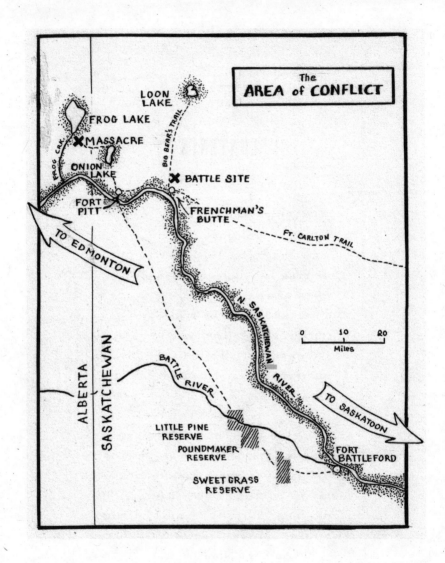

The
AREA of CONFLICT

LOON LAKE

FROG LAKE

✗ MASSACRE

ONION LAKE

FROG CRK.

Big Bear's Trail

✗ BATTLE SITE

FORT PITT

FRENCHMAN'S BUTTE

Ft. CARLTON TRAIL

TO EDMONTON

N. SASKATCHEWAN RIVER

0   10   20
Miles

ALBERTA

SASKATCHEWAN

BATTLE RIVER

TO SASKATOON

LITTLE PINE RESERVE

POUNDMAKER RESERVE

SWEET GRASS RESERVE

FORT BATTLEFORD

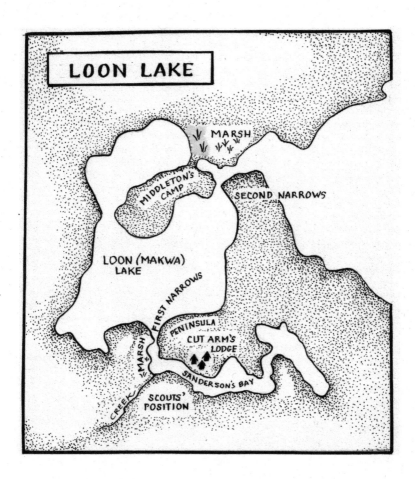

"You Anglo-Saxon people, who have never called any man or nation 'Master,' who since the days of the Norman Kings have never had other manners and customs forced upon you—how can you understand?"

—Edward Ahenakew, *Voices of the Plains Cree*

Prologue

FROG LAKE, ALBERTA, JUNE 9, 1925

Eight graves. Seven metal crosses and one headstone. Only the two priests were missing, buried in another holy place by their church. Near the markers was a newly constructed cairn, a truncated pyramid perhaps a dozen feet tall, built of stones set in mortar on a concrete base. A Union Jack, draped over its face, billowed in the light breeze. Bill Cameron and I stood on either side, waiting to pull the lanyards that would drop the flag and reveal the bronze plaque commemorating those who died there 40 years before.

Several government dignitaries, a few clergymen and a small crowd—adults and children, both white and Native—had gathered for the ceremony. Men who knew nothing of the incident, save what they had read in historical documents, made speeches. One of the clergymen, a Cree, was the last to speak.

"The sun has set on the days of the Indian," he began, "and we still mourn them. Their council fires have gone cold and no one listens to them anymore. But if we are to understand what took place here, some things have to be taken into account." He went on, explaining, not justifying, pleading for understanding, not forgiveness, etching his closing words in my memory. "Imagine them as hunters one day and farmers the next. Imagine them free to roam where they pleased. Then imagine them chained. That is the story of the Indian. And who among us would not rise up in the face of such losses?"

Cameron and I tugged on the lanyards and the flag slid down. There was a smattering of applause. The formal part of the ceremony over, we stood there by those graves, containing bones that once wore the flesh and blood of old friends, as people approached, tentatively at first, and began asking questions.

"What was it like?" they wanted to know, an unkind question asked with little forethought because to them, the massacre was merely history, not experience.

But how could we answer it? What could be said in that place, at that time, that would give them even an inkling of what it had been like?

It would need a book.

ONE

The Stump

I AWOKE WITH SOMETHING wet sliding across my face and a monstrous thirst, my head pounding like a 10-stamp mill. At first, I didn't know where I was but I knew it wasn't in bed at the hotel. My mind gained some focus and I realized I was at the tree stump in front of the jail. The wet thing on my face was the tongue of a small mongrel dog. I shooed it away and made an effort to get up, but when I tried to move my right leg, something held me fast, scraping harshly against my ankle and hurting like hell. Through bleary eyes I saw the leg iron with the chain attached to it, secured by a large spike driven deep into the stump. Now I knew exactly where I was. I managed to get up on my hands and knees before I threw up. It smelled like whisky gone sour because that's exactly what it was.

I heard a noise behind me and turned to see a one-armed, fierce-looking man striding toward me, carrying a bucket of water. I knew his name was John Clough, and that he was a reformed drunkard. He had spent so much time in the local jail that he became the jailer once he decided that sobering up was a damned sight better than being locked up. Using his knee to lift the bottom of the bucket, he grasped the rim with the hand that gripped the bail and emptied the contents all over me. I gasped and spat, and shook my head, which hurt so much that I thought it might come off. I pushed myself up onto my knees and sat back on my calves, rubbing the water from my eyes and gulping shallow breaths. I had never been so humiliated in my life. I was no better than my father and the thought filled me with revulsion. Thank God, my mother couldn't see me; it might have destroyed her.

LESS THAN a day and a half before, I had been in Victoria, hurrying home after work at Saunders' Emporium, along boardwalks and dusty streets in the mid-June sunshine. Ma would need help with the laundry service she provided from our house—wood chopped for the fire and water drawn for the big wooden tubs she kept on the back stoop, one for washing and one for rinsing. The screen door banged shut behind me as I barged in with all the subtlety of youth, glad that a day of paid work was behind me. My arrival home usually brought a smile to Ma's face but not on this day. I could smell the reason why. My father was home.

If you caught my father on one of his sober days you might like him, though he was a stern man. He could smile and when he did his face was kind—some would call it handsome, long after the drink had caused it to sag. But when he was drinking, you didn't have to be in his presence long to know that he could be downright ugly. And he drank most of the time. He was well known in the bars of Victoria's underbelly, and more than a few people who haunted those places feared him. As I did.

Pa was from Philadelphia and had served with the Union Army during the American Civil War. At least that's what he told Ma when they first met; he never spoke to me about it. He never spoke of his family either. As far as I knew, my father's side of our family began with him and ended with me. His name was Caleb Caine, as was mine—Ma called him Cal and me Caleb, so as not to mix us up—but I sometimes wondered if it was fictitious and if he was a deserter.

I did not understand why she put up with him after he became abusive, and would not for many years. I assumed initially that it might be because he had offered Ma her only refuge from a spinster's lonely life, and she grabbed it and hung on, heedless of the cost. It would be just like her to see only her physical plainness and not the beautiful woman she was within. It wasn't until I was much older that I recognized the dogged sense of loyalty in myself and realized where it came from, that I understood why Ma had stuck it out as long as she did.

I don't know that anybody worked harder than Ma did, certainly not my father, who was a common labourer when he was sober enough to work. And since he spent all of his earnings on whisky, Ma cleaned other people's houses and took in laundry to make ends meet, and sometimes just to put food on the table. Her hands were as red as cooked crab and as rough as a cat's tongue though she treated them daily with a variety of liniments. In winter, the kitchen and parlour were crammed with drying racks and the house was insufferably hot. The woodstove burned constantly, heating water, even at the height of summer. In our back yard there were neither trees nor a garden, but posts and ropes with clothes pegs from which she hung the results of her labour out to dry, when it wasn't raining. Once, my father came home in a rage, tore some of the clothes from the lines and stomped them into the dirt. My mother said nothing, only waited until he had passed out in bed, then gathered the clothes and washed them again. In the morning, my father did not remember what he had done and Ma didn't remind him. Though she never said as much, I think she was afraid of what he might do the next time he was drunk.

As I came in, he was sitting at the kitchen table drinking whisky. I wanted to talk to him but said nothing because that's all he wanted from me. Anything else and I was more apt to get the back of his hand, so I went outside to do my chores. It wasn't long before he lurched off to pass out on the bed and Ma called me in to eat.

We sat down to a dinner of boiled potatoes and cabbage with sausages and homemade soda bread. Ma looked tired. There were dark smudges beneath her eyes and she just picked at her food. We talked of wishes and things that might never be, and we talked of my father, snoring loudly in the other room. She was always trying to explain his behaviour. She had told me several times that he was at the Battle of Bull Run, one of the first big battles of the Civil War.

"Your father saw horrific things in the war, Caleb, and he

was no more than a child given a rifle to shoot at other children. He saw the heads of his friends blown off their shoulders, and other men fall around him with their insides hanging out, screaming for their mothers. That has to affect a man, no matter how tough he thinks he is."

But I was too young and distanced from death to see it then. All I saw was how he treated Ma and me. From my perspective, he was the playwright and principal actor of the great tragedy that was his life. And it was a sorrowful thing that Ma and I had supporting roles.

Afterward, I helped her clean up and bring in the wash from the lines out back and while she ironed, I sat with her and we talked some more. Just after dark, we heard Pa stirring.

He came into the kitchen in a foul mood, looking for a drink. Ma had learned a long time ago not to put his whisky where he couldn't find it and had left the bottle in plain sight on the counter near the cups. He went straight to it, grabbed a cup and with a shaking hand poured a generous measure. The best thing for me to do was to be out of his sight, so I went to my room and shut the door.

There was a time when such things upset me terribly but I was beyond that by then. Yet I always experienced a deep sadness and disappointment, not for what Pa was but for what he wasn't—a father I could look up to. And what boy doesn't need that?

I lay on my bed and picked up a dog-eared dime western from a small pile I kept nearby. It was *Wild Jack Strong: Indian Fighter*, in which straight-shootin', straight-talkin' Jack risks his scalp several times to save two friends, a mother and a daughter, kidnapped by a band of savage Indians. At one point, out of bullets and outnumbered, he's nearly captured himself, but beats off the tomahawk-armed Indians with the butt end of his rifle. I don't need to tell you that things turned out for the best. You could depend on it when Wild Jack was around.

I owned all of the Wild Jack Strong books and had read and reread them several times. They gave me places to escape to when my father was drunk, made me dream of being a cowboy. Most boys want to grow up to be like their fathers but I wanted to be like Wild Jack. Now there was a man you could look up to.

I must have slipped into one of those dreams because I was single-handedly turning a herd of stampeding cattle about to trample a beautiful girl, when I heard a voice that didn't belong there. I was confused at first, then I recognized it. It was Ma's voice. And it was heavy with fear.

"Let me go, Cal! You're hurting me!" she cried. I leaped from the bed and rushed into the kitchen. My father had Ma by the arm and she was trying to pry his hand away. "You bitch!" he snarled, and slapped her hard across the face. I went wild.

"Let her go!" I screamed, my fists clenched threateningly. Part of me wanted to hit him for what he was doing to my mother and part of me couldn't because he was my father, a man I'd been afraid of most of my life. But he let go of Ma, who tumbled to the floor, then stuck a long arm out and stopped me cold. While I had his height, I hadn't his weight and wasn't yet his match for strength. With a closed fist, he knocked me clear across the room. I bounced off the wall and flopped to the floor, my head spinning so violently that I nearly vomited.

When I returned to my senses I wanted to cry, not because of the pain in my face but the pain of what a man had done to his wife and son. But I didn't. He already had one kind of a power over me; I would not give him another. I think, in that split-second, if I'd had a gun I might have shot him, even knowing it would have been pure folly. The police frowned on people taking the law into their own hands and I would have gone to jail for it, maybe even been strung up, and that would have been just like Pa reaching a cold hand from the grave to strangle me. I heard the front door slam, which usually meant that he wouldn't be back until the early hours of the morning, if at all. A flood of relief washed over me. Ma came and helped me up.

"Oh, Caleb," she said. "I'm so sorry." Her cheeks were wet with tears and a tiny stream of blood trickled from her nose. She wiped it away with one corner of her apron and used the other to dab her eyes.

"You've got nothing to be sorry about, Ma. It's not your fault." We held each other a long time until finally I said, "I'm leaving, Ma. I don't belong here anymore and I don't want to stay in the same house with him. Come with me. Let's go some place where he'll never find us."

"I can't leave him, Caleb," she said. "I can't desert him. What would he do without me?"

"Don't worry, Ma. He'll find somebody else to knock around. Let's just go. Please!"

"But where to, Caleb? No. This is my home and I'm not leaving it. Pray that your father will come to his senses."

"I'm not sure he has any to come to," I said bitterly. "And I'm not waiting around to find out."

"But where will you go? Where will you sleep tonight?"

"I don't know but it won't be anywhere near this house."

I went to my room and threw some things in a carpetbag. I had a few dollars in a Mason jar that I kept under the bed, out of my father's sight, and I stuffed them into my pocket. In the time it took me to do that I'd pretty much made up my mind where I was going: the mainland. I had enough money to get at least that far and I'd play things by ear from there. Maybe I'd head up to the interior and find work on a ranch.

When I came out, Ma was busying herself in the kitchen. She had put together a small package of food for me and I stowed it in my bag. I gave her a hug and kissed her forehead. She clung to me as if I were a life preserver and part of me hoped she would beg me to stay so that she wouldn't have to face my father by herself. But Ma had too much courage for that. She placed her hands gently on my cheeks and said only, "You're a fine young man, Caleb, and I don't blame you for leaving. It may be time for you to be on your own anyway. Just look after yourself and come back to me safely. And don't forget to write."

"I won't, Ma, I promise."

She went to a cupboard and from the top shelf retrieved a small canister. "I have something for you." Inside was money in bills and coins. She took out all the bills and put them into my hand. "Take this," she said.

It was rainy-day money she had managed to put aside and I didn't want to take it. She could see I had misgivings but closed my fist around the wad and squeezed tightly.

"Don't be silly, now," she said, before I could protest. "You'll need it. Besides, you've earned it with all the work you've done around here."

I reluctantly shoved it into my pocket. "Thanks, Ma," I said. I told her that the Emporium owed me three days' pay and that she should get it from Mr. Saunders the next time she was downtown. "He'll understand," I added. He knew the kind of man my father was.

I kissed her damp cheek and she followed me to the door and stood there, a dark silhouette against the lamplight, as I walked out the gate. I hated leaving her but we all have to make choices and she had made hers. At least that's how I've explained it to myself over the years. If it was cruel I can only say that most young men are not blessed with the gift of understanding someone else's tears better than their own.

CLOUGH SQUATTED and stuck his ugly face in mine. He had a gap between his tobacco-stained front teeth wide enough to ride a pony through. His voice was rough and phlegmy and his breath smelled as foul as an overused privy. I wanted to throw up again.

"So, you're alive, laddie," he said "You don't deserve to be."

He was right. I didn't. Not if there was any truth to the memories of the night before that were slowly taking shape in my foggy brain. I remembered the size of the man I tried to pick a fight with but I couldn't remember if I had been knocked out or had just passed out. My jaw and nose were intact and felt unbruised, so it must have been the latter. Anyway, that's why I was chained to this stump in the street. It was how the community of Gastown punished drunks for their first offence. When I passed out, they must have sent for Clough. Whatever the case, I was his prisoner and I begged him to turn me loose, vowing that I was properly ashamed and would never do it again.

"That was my story," he said. "That's the one I always told and I don't recall giving you permission to use it."

"I'm sorry if I used your story," I whined. "I didn't mean to. It was all I could think of to say. I'll never do it again, honest!"

"Well, not until suppertime anyway," he said. "The only drink we serve at the stump is water and this is where you'll be spending the rest of the day. I've spent some time here myself, laddie, and I tell you, a day here in plain view of the townsfolk is a grand way to make you put some commitment behind your words. I'll see you at lunch with some bread and water."

He picked up the bucket and sauntered over to the jail. I don't know who I hated more, that gap-toothed, reformed drunk or myself for getting into this mess.

TWO

Rites of Passage

I HAD ARRIVED IN GASTOWN the night before, just at dinner time, and had gone straight to the Sunnyside Hotel. It was a whitewashed building jutting out over the waters of Burrard Inlet on pilings, with its name in black lettering across the top at the front. The lobby was utilitarian with the front desk built of local lumber, sanded and oiled—nothing elaborate. To the right of the lobby, past the stairs to the rooms above, was the dining area, a square space that contained only one long table with a dozen chairs around it. A large window provided a fine view of the harbour and the north shore mountains, where two nearly identical peaks rose up behind the lower ones; the local, female-starved, male population had lewdly dubbed them "Sheba's Tits."

In behind the dining room and lobby, running the width of both, was a barroom. Several round tables and chairs adorned the floor and there was a billiards table in one corner. A passage led from behind the bar to the front desk and when it wasn't busy, the same man ran both stations.

A burly black man was working the desk. He spoke with an accent that I later learned was Caribbean, and was polite and generous with his smiles. Even better, his eyes did not acknowledge that one of mine was bruised black.

"Yes, sir," he said. "Can I help you?"

"Yes, I, uh, would like a room for the night." I had never uttered such words before and they seemed strange coming from my mouth, as if someone else were speaking them. "Maybe tomorrow night too," I quickly added.

He pulled the register over. "Yes, sir. If you'll just sign here."

I took the pen from its holder and signed, "Jack Strong."

I have no idea what possessed me to write that name down as mine but I did not feel like myself. Maybe it was the black eye and the need to be someone much stronger than I felt. Or maybe it was just the fantasies playing around in my head. Whatever it was, the more I ran it through my mind, the more I believed it to be an idea with merit. It was a man's name, a name with power and a good one to live up to. More important, it wasn't my father's. It would be mine from now on, and the thought ignited a fire in my gut. I could feel its heat building up into my chest.

I chatted for a few moments with the black man, who said to call him "Joe," and asked if he knew of any jobs around.

"Best try the mill," he said. "They always seem to be hirin', especially this time of year, with summer coming on."

He was referring to Hastings Mill, a smoking hodgepodge of buildings about a half mile up the inlet.

"There's loggin' camps around, too," he added. "There's loggers stayin' at the hotel and you can talk to them if you've a mind to. You might catch a few of them in the dining room at supper time."

I thanked Joe for the information and took my bag up to my room. I had an hour to kill before dinner, so I went for a walk to stretch my legs and to see what the town was like.

Gastown wasn't much to speak of in 1884 and offered few clues that it would one day become the metropolis of Vancouver. But considering the size of the place, there were plenty of people on the boardwalks. There were Chinese, Indians, even a couple of blacks, but most of the people I passed were white and predominantly male. Gastown itself had only a couple of hundred inhabitants, including those who lived at the Hastings Mill site, but crews from ships idle in the harbour, and from logging camps in the vicinity, helped fill the streets and saloons, and lent the town the air of a much larger, more cosmopolitan place.

A plank road that was half on land and half over the beach led west past nondescript, wood-frame buildings among which were a saloon, a dry-goods store and a Chinese laundry. At the west end of town there were a few houses and a Methodist church; below that floated a large boathouse. At this point, the boardwalk ended and a trail continued above the beach. Another well-used trail went off into a salal-choked forest. Gastown's only other thoroughfare, Water Street, took me back in the direction from which I had just come, behind all the buildings I'd passed on the way. Its south side was lined with more frame structures, backed by a thin line of conifers through which I caught glimpses of a large tract of stump-ridden land and blackberry bushes. I passed a general store and a few more stumps along the way, one near the courthouse and jail that had a chain and manacle bolted to it. The street ended at a giant old maple tree in front of Gassy Jack's Saloon. On the north side of the tree was the rear of the Sunnyside Hotel. A skid road that seemed to rise out of the water ran at an acute angle into the woods.

Leading off to the east was the boardwalk that linked Gastown to Hastings Mill; it sat squat and ugly against the heavily treed north shore mountains angling off into the distance. Plumes of smoke billowed up from two large stacks and a thimble-shaped refuse burner, and drifted in a pall across the inlet. It was like a cold sore on the lips of a beautiful woman; nevertheless, the mill was the primary reason Gastown existed.

I returned to the hotel for dinner. I would have felt content but I couldn't help wondering how Ma was doing.

The all-male gathering around the dining table was rough-looking, loggers in town for Saturday night fun and, for some, church the next morning. The place reeked of masculinity and toilet water. A couple of the men were attired in frayed black suits with once-white shirts that cried out for a visit to the Chinese laundry. Others simply wore wide suspenders over their shirts, but to a man, they appeared to be a hardworking lot, with calloused hands and weather-burnished faces that sported goatees, full beards or great drooping moustaches.

I entered the room to the sound of knives and forks scraping on china, and conversation came to a halt as I walked to the far end of the table and sat down. I could feel everyone's eyes turn my way but I wasn't about to let it intimidate me.

"Evening," I ventured. There were nods of hello and murmured greetings, and conversation resumed. Sitting next to me was a burly man with a grey-flecked, bushy beard and a bit of the jokester in his lively blue eyes. He asked, "Where ya from?" He spoke in a kind of growl that made me want to clear my throat.

"Victoria."

He grunted. "Spent a week there one night," he said, shoving a fork full of roast beef into his mouth. He chewed for a while, then asked, "What brings ya to this neck of the woods?"

"I'm looking for work."

He eyed me with a bit of a squint, as if he were taking my measure. "Ever worked in a loggin' operation before?"

I shook my head. "I think I'll try the mill. See if I can get hired on there."

"Ya probably will. They're always lookin' for men and ye're a big strappin' lad. But I'll tell ya somethin', ya work for them an' they own ya. They don't like ya spendin' yer money anywhere but at the mill store. They don't like ya drinkin' there either." He jammed a large chunk of potato in his mouth, barely seemed to chew it, and said, "I own a loggin' operation over False Creek way. We need young blood from time to time, so if things don't work out at the mill, come and see me. Maybe we'll have somethin'. The pay may not be as good but at least ya'd be more yer own man."

"Thanks," I said. "I appreciate the offer."

He shrugged and stuck out his hand. "Pete Thomson."

"Pleased to know you, Pete," I said. His hand was like fir bark. "Jack Strong."

"Oh, yah?" said Pete, his face lighting up with a knowing grin. "Wild Jack, eh? I had you pegged for a much older man."

It was plain that Pete considered himself the owner of a fine sense of humour but I should have known that sooner or later, the name would evoke such a response. If I wanted to keep it, I was going to have to get used to the good-natured ribbing.

After an adequate dinner—Pete put away enough food to keep me stoked for two or three days, and I was no slouch—he asked, "Buy you a drink, Wild Jack?"

"Sure," I said as casually as I could. To be truthful, it made me nervous but if I wanted to call myself a man, the bar was as appropriate a place as any to start. Drinking was one of the rituals that defined masculinity, especially in places like Gastown. The trick was not to let it get the best of you, as it had my father.

I followed Pete into the bar as he let out a loud belch. "Whisky?" he asked and I nodded. I found a seat over by the billiards table while Pete went to get our drinks. The place was busy. Noisy, too, with the sound of men trying to talk over one another and the clack of billiard balls. Pete came back with doubles and raised his glass. "Drink up, kid," he said. "If you've come here to do a man's work, you might as well have a man's fun."

I didn't like being called "kid" but didn't say anything,

just hoisted the glass. I had never touched liquor before and nearly choked on the first sip, which seemed to go up into my nose before it went down into my belly. It tasted bloody awful but I tried not to grimace. Then it generated a warm glow in my gut, and a feeling of well-being and confidence surged through me. The hard edges of the world softened and all of the doubts and fears I'd had about leaving home disappeared like summer fog. Were these the feelings my father was always searching for? The second swallow went down a whole lot easier and if I hadn't had a belly full of food I think I might have been on the floor with that first glass.

Pete hailed from California and had first come north when gold was discovered in the Cariboo in 1862. He returned home empty-handed and found work as a logger for a few years until a friend talked him into coming to Burrard Inlet. He worked at Hastings Mill for a while but hated being a company man and soon started his own logging operation. The high demand around the world for the timber from this area kept him busy.

Pete seemed happy to have someone listen to the same things he'd most likely said a thousand times before, and bought another round. He told me more about Gastown, or Granville as it was more properly known. "Only the high-brows in town and out at the mill call it Granville," he said. "They'd like it ta be somethin' more than it is but if ya think of the mill as a church and Gastown as a whorehouse, it'll give ya a pretty good idea about the difference between the two places. I've bin in these parts for nearly 15 years and I haven't seen a single mill manager that hasn't been some kinda fuckin' moral tyrant. And Alexander McRae, the guy who manages it now, ain't any different."

Pete rambled on about the town, the mill and some of the people around, while I sipped at my whisky until the room started to spin. It was hot in the bar and there was enough smoke in the place to rival the refuse burner over at the mill. I told Pete I needed some air.

"Whisky gettin' to ya, Wild Jack? Maybe we oughta go for a ride," Pete said, the jokester dancing in his eyes.

"You got a wagon or horses or something?" I asked.

He roared with laughter and clapped me on the shoulder. "Shit, Wild Jack. Tell me you've screwed something more than your hand at least once in your life!"

When I didn't answer, he looked me up and down and added, "Well, better late than never. A boy can't rightly call himself a man until he's had his first poke."

I sensed the truth in what he was saying and the whisky made me feel reckless. "What are we sitting here for?" I asked, trying not to slur my words.

"Now ye're on the right track," he said.

We left the bar and walked down the boardwalk along the waterfront. I was a little unsteady on my feet. It was still light, as the sun had only just disappeared behind the trees to the west. The sky was cloudless, the water flat calm. Many people, whose custom was not a night in the bar, were out on their porches enjoying the warm evening. Away from the stale air and smoke, my head began to clear and I asked Pete where we were going.

"Not far. The place belongs to a couple of klootches.

Sisters, and pretty as fresh paint. It's early enough that they shouldn't be busy. By the way, how'd ya get the shiner? It's a beauty."

I wondered what had taken Pete so long to ask because there was nothing about him that even remotely suggested a problem with shyness. But if I told him the truth it would require an explanation that I wasn't up to providing, so I simply said, "A horse banged me with its muzzle."

"Sure," Pete said. He knew he wasn't getting a straight answer but did not pursue it.

We continued along the boardwalk, past the Methodist church, and went into the forest along a wide and well-trodden path that cut through the salal and snaked past a small bog leafy with skunk cabbage. After a few minutes, we came to a smaller trail that branched off to the left and led to a clearing containing a shack so crudely built that blind men might have thrown it together.

Pete didn't bother to knock but pushed the door open on squawking hinges. We strode into a dingy room furnished only with a stove and a plank table surrounded by a few dilapidated chairs. Two doorways, covered by burlap, led off the back wall. A half-light came in through two small, dirty windows and an oil lamp guttered low on the table at which sat two women of indeterminate age. Both were thickset beneath loose cotton frocks, and wore their raven hair tied up in a bun. They were rather pretty despite bad teeth, apparent in the broad smiles they had for Pete.

"Kla-how-ya," he said.

"Kla-how-ya," the women replied in unison.

Pete spoke to them in Chinook, the trade language along the coast. I didn't understand a single word but it seemed as if he was bargaining with one of them on my behalf because she kept glancing over at me. He gave a negative shake to his head, which I guessed would only save me money.

Despite being mildly intoxicated, I was aware of my heart pounding against my ribs. I couldn't believe where I was; Victoria and home seemed on the far side of the world. "What's she saying?" I asked Pete, growing impatient. I didn't like being outside the conversation.

"She's askin' if ye're my son and if I've brought ya here for yer first poke."

I must have blushed because the woman giggled. "Just ask her how much she wants," I said eagerly.

"That's what I bin tryin' ta work out, if ya'll give me a minute."

He spoke to her again, then turned to me. "Two dollars," he said. "She's givin' you a bargain cuz yer so young and she don't think ya'll waste much of her time."

She reached out her hand to me, rubbing her thumb against her fingers. "Chickimin, chickimin." She repeated the word a couple more times.

I looked at Pete questioningly.

"She wants her money now," Pete translated.

I suppose I should have felt insulted, but I didn't. I grinned inanely, all set to prove her wrong. I gave her the money and, taking my hand, she led me through one of the burlap curtains. While I tagged along behind her like a pup on a leash, Pete went through the other curtain with his woman. I noticed that he didn't have to pay up front.

Another low-burning lamp sat on a small table that was just a couple of sawed-off planks nailed to a stump. A cot was sandwiched between it and the wall, and there wasn't much else in the room: neither a window nor a picture for decoration. The place had an unusual smell that I couldn't identify. The woman lay on her back on the bed and without ceremony hitched up her dress and spread her legs. The black, hairy mound of her crotch was not like anything I had ever imagined but it possessed secrets, about to be revealed. So while my mind was wondering what all the fuss had been about, my nether region was rising to the cause.

She motioned me onto the bed. I climbed on and got on my knees between her legs, pulling my suspenders off my shoulders and fumbling at the buttons on my trousers. My fingers had somehow lost their dexterity, so she brushed my hands aside and finished the job herself, which aroused me even further. I grabbed her melon breasts through her dress but she pushed my hands away and said something, maybe that they weren't included in the price. I noticed a smell of old fish about her and I was too nervous and naïve to tell if it came from that dark mound or her breath, but I soon ceased to care. She lay there as lively as the stump beside the bed, a mere receptacle, while I poked and prodded until I found my way inside her. For a few moments, I believed she was the most beautiful creature in the world but, just as she predicted, I hadn't wasted her time. I was finished.

My lust sated, I had a driving need to get out of there. I did myself up and pulled on my suspenders. I wondered where I'd put my cap until I realized that I hadn't even taken it off. I told the woman goodbye, which she acknowledged with a grunt as she pulled her dress down. I left amid sounds of wild thrashings from the adjacent room. Pete was apparently a man of some experience.

Despite the short-lived nature of the venture, which I could ill afford, I figured it was two dollars well spent. The woman, combined with the whisky beforehand, was as valid a rite of passage as any young man could experience and I felt a completely changed person. It blended well with my new image. I seemed to float above the ground as I made my way along the trail and I reached Water Street feeling that the world was a much improved place over the night before.

It's funny how some activities demand tea afterward, or coffee or sarsaparilla, while others require whisky. When I came to the first saloon I saw no need to go any farther. It was a grotty, noisy little place with smoke nearly down to the floor. There was a space at the bar and I bellied up to it like the man I'd become. "Whisky," I told the bartender, trying to make my voice sound deeper than it was. "Make it a double." I plunked a dollar onto the bar. I could have crowed, I was so elated.

I don't know how many drinks I had, only that after a while the people around me began to recede in my vision. Sweat broke out on my forehead. I felt a little wobbly and had to hold onto the bar to steady myself. It would have been better to go back to the hotel right then and there but good sense has never stood in youth's way for fear of being trampled. A big man standing next to me told me that if I wanted another drink maybe I should go home and suck on my mother's tit. The whisky had robbed me of any discretion I might have had when sober and though the man didn't look anything like my father, he was a good enough substitute. I took a swing at him. And that's the last thing I remembered.

THE SUN rose and beat down on me relentlessly. I couldn't escape it, and wouldn't until the afternoon when the stump itself would provide some shade. Pete showed up with rheumy eyes and a colossal hangover. He hunkered down and grinned. "Mornin', Wild Jack," he said. "I see it didn't take ya long to meet One-Arm John."

"You seem really concerned, Pete," I grumbled.

"Ya didn't stay long at the shack last night." His grin widened.

"I got my two dollars' worth."

"Great! It'd grieve me no end if ya hadn't."

He laughed and clapped my shoulder, which made my head throb.

"Oh," I moaned. "Don't do that!"

"I'm headin' back ta camp. If ya want work, come on out when ye're done here. Just follow the skids on the other side of Gassy Jack's, on out to False Creek. We ain't hard to find."

"Jeez, thanks, Pete," I said, "but what I really need is to get out of here. Is there any way you can help me? Maybe if you talk to One-Arm John he'll let me go."

I was whining again and knew it but couldn't help myself.

"The only thing that'll get ya outta here is to be quiet and take yer medicine. I can tell ya that from experience. But think pretty thoughts, my friend, and the day'll be gone before ya know it. See ya." He paused, tugging at his cap brim, another grin flooding his face, and added, "Wild Jack." Then he was off down the street.

Wild Jack. I was an embarrassment to the name and despised myself for it.

Luckily, as it was Sunday morning there weren't many people on the street and for that I was grateful. I even managed to doze off for a while. But the sun hadn't reached its zenith when the street began to get busier. The Methodist church emptied out and most of its parishioners passed the stump, ogling me. I wanted to crawl into a hole and cover myself up. One family—the parents, two small boys and a gorgeous teenaged daughter—stared at me particularly hard, as if they were truly offended by my presence at the stump. The man, who was well dressed, had piercing blue eyes that burned into me and forced my gaze down.

I had no doubt that I was the most conspicuous human being on the planet until One-Arm John came at 5:00 P.M. to unchain me. I was weak with relief that the ordeal was finally over and resolved that I would never place myself in such a position again. I didn't thank Clough and headed straight for the hotel to get some supper, glad that it wasn't far from the stump.

Joe was working the front desk again and greeted me with that charming smile of his. I expected him to pass some comment about my stint at the stump but all he said was, "Ah, Mr. Strong."

I liked the sound of that but didn't exactly feel I was worthy of such respect. He had saved my room for me, so I

paid for another night and went upstairs. I was ashamed of
what I saw in the mirror. Ma had always said that I had my
father's handsomeness but I resembled him now in ways I
didn't care to think about. I smelled terrible, too. I filled the
bowl on the sideboard with water from the pitcher next to it,
stripped naked and scrubbed myself clean. I towelled myself
dry, put on clean clothes and went down to an almost empty
dining room. Most of the guests from the night before had
returned to the camps so I had a quiet dinner. Afterward, I
crawled into bed and slept the evening and night away.

First thing in the morning I headed out to the mill, but
not without some trepidation. I was nervous about seeing the
manager. It would be a miracle if he hadn't heard about my
misadventures and, after what Pete had said about his moral
tyranny, I doubted that I was the kind of employee he'd want
to hire.

Every time I met someone on the narrow boardwalk I felt
acutely embarrassed, certain that they knew about me. I
passed the entrance to the dock where stevedores were loading
huge timbers through hatches on either side of the bow of a
ship nosed into the dock, manhandling them with grappling
hooks and peaveys. All the men looked tough and lean, and I
wondered if I could handle a job like that if I were lucky
enough to get hired on. The hardest work I'd ever done was
move light merchandise around in a dry-goods store.

The air was relatively fresh, as the prevailing wind was
blowing the burner smoke up the inlet for others to breathe.
It was a gloriously warm day and the front door to the mill
office was wide open. I told the clerk my name and why I had

come, and, with the superiority many clerks think they have over everyone but their bosses, he instructed me to have a chair and wait.

He disappeared into an inner office and returned moments later. "Mr. McRae will see you now," he said, the tone in his voice hinting that I just might be the luckiest person in the world.

When I saw McRae, I almost fell over. His eyebrows shot up at my entrance and those piercing blue eyes from yesterday locked onto mine and drilled holes right through me.

"Ah," he said, not without an element of disgust in his voice. "The young man from the stump."

THREE

Atonement

THE OFFICE WAS SPACIOUS BUT austere, the walls bare except for two pictures: one of the mill and the other of Queen Victoria. The only furniture was McRae's desk and chair, and a few other chairs perhaps used for meetings. Nothing in the place suggested comfort and McRae seemed like the kind of man who had little time for it.

He was probably in his late 30s, his dark hair and bushy moustache flecked lightly with grey. His eyes, deep-set in a handsome face, reflected an ample intelligence, and he exuded confidence and competence. His deep voice, serious demeanour and Scots accent added to his authoritative air.

I knew I was a sight. The bruise around my eye had turned purple and yellow, and the fact that he and his family had seen me at my worst made me feel awkward and ashamed. There was a straight-back, wooden chair in front of his desk but he didn't ask me to sit down. His eyes burned into me for an eternity—Pete had said it was how he controlled every conversation—before he spoke.

"My clerk tells me you're looking for work, Mr. Strong." He didn't pause to let me answer and went on, the words hard as ice. "But I would be doing the mill a disservice if I took you on. In our brief encounter you did not leave a very good impression, which is the kindest thing I can say. You might find work in one of the logging camps in the area, although some of those men can be downright barbaric at times and we wouldn't want to see any of that rub off on you, would we?"

"I, uh . . ." I was going to apologize but he didn't let me get the words out.

"Good day, Mr. Strong. Please close the door on your way out. *Silently* if you will."

Insulted and angry, I spun on my heels and stomped out the door, slamming it shut so hard it shook the building and presumably ended any future chance I might have had of getting hired at the mill. I stormed past the clerk, who had a shocked look on his face, and fumed all the way back to Gastown.

All I really wanted to do at that point was to leave town at the first opportunity but that would have been like running away and I wasn't about to run from anyone. Besides, I needed money. I considered heading out to False Creek to take Pete up on his offer but that would have been like hiding and I wasn't going to hide from anyone either. As it turned out, Joe provided a solution.

He could sense my anger and mortification, and easily guessed the cause of it. He asked how I was doing and since it needed venting, I flat out told him, trying not to be too vitriolic about it.

"Mr. McRae can be a hard man to please and that's a fact," he said. "But maybe things ain't as bad as you think."

It so happened that the Sunnyside needed a roustabout because the regular man had quit. Joe led me to the owner's office and introduced me. Mr. Meany, a rotund, jovial man the opposite of his name, wasn't anywhere near as particular as McRae. He offered to hire me on the spot provided I could start right away. I would be cleaning up the dining room and the bar, washing dishes, making sure there was plenty of water on hand in the rooms and splitting wood when it was needed. The work was menial, the pay poor, but it included all meals and that was no small bonus. Unfortunately, it didn't include accommodations and on my pay I couldn't afford the Sunnyside. Joe came to my rescue again.

He owned a small house at the west end of Water Street. It had four rooms and I could have one for a small fee until I found something else. His major concern was that I keep it clean and contribute to the ongoing maintenance of the house. Joe was an orderly man; I could see that by how neatly he dressed. But Ma was orderly too, and had always insisted that I keep my room clean, so I was accustomed to the task.

"I can do that," I said.

I hastened up to the hotel room, fetched my bag, stowed it behind Joe's desk and went to work, washing dishes.

To some degree I was wary that there might be strings

attached to Joe's offer—men who were fond of younger members of their own sex were not uncommon—but my suspicions were unfounded. Joe Fortes never tied a string to anyone; he was just that kind of man and he would have made the same offer to any person he considered in need of his help.

He was broad of shoulder, a couple of inches shorter than my six feet, and was blessed with one of the most engaging smiles I've ever seen on a man. It seemed to come from every muscle in his face, and his dark eyes gleamed. He was also easier to get along with than anyone I'd ever met. And he never once brought up my punishment at the stump except to say that he never drank and did not want liquor in his house.

"It ain't up to me to tell a man how to live, Jack," he said later, "but that stuff you was drinkin' is poison. Any man with an ounce of sense wouldn't touch it an' I think you got sense. You made a mistake, that's all. I could tell the first day you walked into the hotel that there was nothin' bad about you, even though you looked a little roughed up. I ain't never been wrong yet and I don't expect I am this time."

That first night at his place we got to know each other better. He was as curious about me as I was about him. I'd seen black people before, on the streets of Victoria, but I had never sat down and talked with one. I'd be a liar if I said it didn't seem strange at first but the man inside Joe made you quickly forget the man on the outside.

After dinner we sat on his front porch drinking coffee, enjoying the dregs of the pot and the day. I was more relaxed than I had been for some time. We made a fine pair, Joe and I. He was a bit of an outcast because of his colour, and I was one because of my stupidity, and there were more than a few people in town who believed that any man low enough to end up at the stump was well suited to living with a black man. But Joe knew himself too well to pay any attention to such people, and some of his self-respect rubbed off on me and allowed me to walk with my head a little higher.

He had been born in Barbados to parents who were the children of slaves and in many ways, given the dependency of the island on sugar cane, were like slaves themselves right up until their deaths. But the French government and the Panama Canal saved Joe from the same fate. He was recruited, along with thousands of other Barbadians, to work on the canal and he went eagerly. He carried lumber until his back ached and he wore the skin off his shoulders, saving some of his pay so that his parents could buy their own house and land and live out their lives independently, free from slave labour. Sadly, they died before he achieved his dream for them, so he used the money instead to buy passage to England.

He ended up in Liverpool and got a job as a bathhouse attendant and swimming instructor. Seeking further adventures, he hired on as a crew member on a cargo ship and worked his way to Gastown where he began work at the Sunnyside Hotel as a roustabout and shoeshine boy. Hard, conscientious work resulted in a job handling the desk and the bar. For the most part, people were friendly to him but few were inclined to be his friend. But that was all right. He knew who he was and what he wanted out of life.

Joe was as happy and generous a man as I had ever met, whose greatest passion in life was swimming. He swam in the harbour every day of the year, regardless of the weather, and gave lessons to all comers whether they could afford to pay him or not. He was one of those good Samaritans in this world who are always willing to give even a stranger a leg up. He was only about 10 years my senior but had the wisdom of someone much older. One of his greatest gifts was accepting people for what they were, not what for what he'd like them to be. As time went on, I told him what I was up to, that I had come to Gastown to find work until I had enough money to get up to the interior and maybe find work on a ranch. Owning a ranch one day was my dream, I confessed, though it had just come to me.

"Nothin' wrong with a man dreamin'," he said, nodding sagely at what he knew was a fundamental truth. "I always had dreams. Still do. Wouldn't be much without 'em."

I even trusted him enough to tell the true story of why I had left home and about the black eye. He took it all in, silently, and in the telling I felt something heavy lift off my heart. When I was done he shook his head slowly and sighed. "It's always best that a man steps out in troubled times, Jack. It's too easy to draw in and hide. You done the right thing, that's for sure."

IT WAS nearing the end of June and I had been at the Sunnyside for about two weeks when I read an article in a week-old newspaper that set me to thinking. It was on the second page but its bold title "INDIAN WAR?" caught my attention. It said that there was concern in Parliament about an uprising on the prairies. The Cree around Fort Battleford were complaining that the government was failing to honour its treaties and they were starving. On June 17, two Indians had gone to their reserve's farm instructor, a man named John Craig, and demanded food. Craig refused. When the Indians persisted, Craig herded them outside. One of the Indians picked up an axe handle and clubbed Craig with it. The instructor was not seriously hurt but reported the incident to the police who went to arrest the culprit. However, Chiefs Big Bear and Poundmaker stepped in and would not allow it. To make matters worse, the Métis along the South Saskatchewan River were dissatisfied with their treatment at the hands of the government, too. There was talk of war among both factions.

If there was going to be a fight, I thought, *why not go join it?* I had showed everyone, including me, my worst side and this could be a way of showing my best. It was also a way of living up to the name of Wild Jack Strong and could prove to be the sort of thing that turns boys into men. And it wouldn't hurt that at the same time, I could show my father I was more of a man than he ever was or could be.

"Good God Almighty, Jack!" Joe cried when I told him I was leaving and where I was going. "Them Indians ain't like the ones we got here. Why, they'd just as soon scalp you as look at you! That ain't no place for a young fella of your quality, I'll tell you that much, my friend."

But I had made up my mind. It was time to move on and make something of myself. I wrote a letter to Ma and told her

I was doing fine and working at the Sunnyside —which wasn't a lie because I hadn't yet quit—and said that I'd be leaving soon to look for ranch work. That wasn't quite a lie; I would do it eventually but she'd worry herself sick if she knew what I was really up to. When I finished I asked Joe to post it for me.

"I'll do that for you, Jack, and more, if you ask."

"I wouldn't ask for another thing, Joe. You've already given me more than enough. I don't know what I would have done without you."

He had been like a brother to me, sometimes a father, and I was about to say so when he interrupted me.

"Don't you go gettin' maudlin on me now, Jack. You just turn around and come back one day when it's time to. And keep that hair of yours on top of your head where it's supposed to be. That's all you need to do for Joe."

When I got my pay from the Sunnyside and tried to give him the money for the room, he refused to take it.

"I got money, Jack. I don't need yours. You got a long way to go and you'll need every penny you got to get there."

I bought a few things I would need for the journey, the most important being extra socks, a knife and matches, and that night packed my bag. Joe gave me a small tarp and a thick wool blanket that he said he no longer needed—they would keep me warm and dry if it rained. The following morning I walked with my friend to the Sunnyside and ate a hearty breakfast of beefsteak and eggs, and stuffed myself with rolls. There were a few extra left on the table and Joe put them in a cotton string bag for me.

We knew instinctively that it would be of no use to either

of us to prolong our goodbyes, so we said them straight up, shook hands and I set out for the mill and the stagecoach to New Westminster. It wasn't until much later in the day, when I got hungry for a roll, that I saw what else Joe had put in the bag: $20, wrapped in a note that read in a barely legible scrawl: "Jack—just in case you run yourself short. Your friend Joe."

FOUR

The Trader

THE FABLED NORTH Saskatchewan River was low and turbid, split here and there by sandbars. On the far bluff was Fort Edmonton, a drab and lonely sentinel. Beyond, on the skyline, was the settlement. We crossed the river on a cable ferry under grey skies and, after dropping some mail off at the fort, drove around a huge house sitting on a knoll and picked up the rutted trail to town.

My first clear impression of the hamlet was neither its buildings nor its people: it was the sound of drums. Indian drums beat on so persistently that I figured I might not need to go all the way to Fort Battleford, where the real trouble was brewing. I figured I was hearing war drums, that I had landed right in the thick of things, yet all the townsfolk seemed unconcerned and were going about their daily business. I asked one of the locals, a well-dressed man, if it meant that the Indians were about to go on the warpath.

"Not at all," he said. "They drum for a lot of reasons." His mouth turned up in a half-smile. "You'll only need to worry if they stop and you find their lodges gone. That usually means they're moving their women and children to a safe place before they attack."

My pulse quickened. Much of the town was built right to the edge of the forest, which seemed risky to me because it would allow the Indians to sneak up undetected. I mentioned this to the man, who nodded.

"Very perceptive. There's talk of clearing a space between the town and the forest but so far no one's got around to it." His eyes swept over me. "You're new around here." It was a statement.

Trying to be matter-of-fact, I said, "I'm from the coast. Just came in on the stage. I read that there might be Indian troubles out this way and I wanted to throw my hand in."

The man clearly wasn't impressed and looked at me askance. "Well, if you don't mind me saying so, a young fella like yourself ought to be able to find better things to do than get himself killed. Any damned fool can do that." He tapped his temple with his index finger. "It takes a smart man to stay alive."

I bristled. "I don't plan on getting myself killed."

He raised his eyebrows and dropped them. "No one ever does. Anyway, if this town is attacked we'll need more help than you can offer."

He went on to explain that the white population in the area numbered only 150 or so, while the Indians and half-breeds numbered in the many hundreds if not thousands.

The encampment that could be seen at the edge of town reflected only a small portion of them; there were many more within just a few miles.

"What about the fort?" I asked.

"The numbers I mentioned included the fort. Besides, it's not a military fort—it's just a Hudson's Bay Company post and it would offer only temporary protection at best. There's a North-West Mounted Police post at Fort Saskatchewan, about 20 miles east of here, but it just has a handful of men. Without reinforcements, the Indians could take us any time they wanted. But I wouldn't worry if I were you. They've always been relatively friendly and they still are, despite the deplorable way the government treats them. You might want to head down to Fort Battleford if you're spoiling for a fight. It's the Cree down there who've been causing most of the trouble."

He tugged on the brim of his hat, wished me well and moved on. I thought he was a strange duck at first, apparently an Indian sympathizer, but when others I spoke to expressed similar viewpoints it occurred to me that what I was hearing was not so much concern for the Indians' welfare as it was concern for themselves, and for what the Indians might do if the government didn't keep its promises.

I still had money left but deemed it wise to keep some in reserve, so I made inquiries around town about temporary work. I came up with nothing. The owner of the general store said it was difficult enough to keep the townsfolk working and suggested that I try the fort. Perhaps the Company could help me out.

The fort was busier than the town. Its high palisades

enclosed a host of buildings and people: whites, Indians, half-breeds and more dogs and excrement than there ought to be in one place at one time. There were even a few red-coated policemen about and one of them directed me to the Company store where he'd just seen the agent enter.

He was easy to pick out, a dour-faced Scotsman oozing authority. He didn't look at all approachable; nevertheless, I went up to him and asked about work.

"Where would ye like to start, lad?" he said without the slightest trace of humour. "It's no less than governor for ye, I'll wager. Leave it with me and I'll see wha' I can do. In the meantime, I'm sure ye'll forgive me when I say that I'm a busy man and have little time for the likes of ye."

He turned away and busied himself perusing a large book that may have been a ledger. There were other people in the store; their eyes bored through me. A couple of them wore grins, clearly enjoying the agent's caustic rebuff. Not knowing how to respond, I turned on my heels and left the store, and went down to the river to lick my wounds.

I had only enough money for a steamer ticket to Fort Battleford, plus a little extra for food, so even if I wanted the comfort of a hotel I couldn't afford it. I set up my bedroll among some bushes on the riverbank. If the Indians did decide to go on the rampage in the middle of the night, they weren't likely to find me down there.

I waited three days for the steamer to arrive from Winnipeg. The weather remained grey, rainy and cool, and though it made whiling away the time tedious, it at least kept the mosquitoes at bay. They can drive a man crazy in that country.

I HEARD the steamboat's shrill whistle and saw her smoke belching skyward long before she finally rounded the bend and tied up below the fort. By then I'd had enough of Edmonton and its fort to last me for a long while.

I was relegated to the lower deck of the SS *Northwest* with a few Métis traders, bales of fur, wooden crates of unknown content and firewood for the ship's boilers. While first-class passengers on the upper deck enjoyed fine food and wine, those below ate beans and biscuits with tea. The traders were friendly and some spoke passable English but not enough to carry on a decent conversation. Nonetheless, they were convivial and offered me rum from a small cask and tobacco, both of which I declined. Memories of the stump were still too fresh in my mind and smoking had never appealed to me. While they weren't insulted by my abstinence, neither were they impressed.

For such a large vessel, the *Northwest* drew less than two feet of water, which made her perfect for the North Saskatchewan. In the dry season the river could be extremely shallow, although recent rains had raised it to a comfortable level, except at one sharp bend far downstream where a sandbar blocked the way. The captain simply turned the boat around and used the big paddle wheel to churn up the sand. Otherwise, the journey was uneventful, the river snaking through the rolling sameness of the prairie. As each day passed the sky grew clearer and the heat more intense, and by the time we reached Fort Battleford, five days later, it was stifling. And we were in the heart of hostile Indian country.

The town sat on a plateau at the junction of the North

Saskatchewan and Battle rivers. Not far away the NWMP post flew the Union Jack and equalled the town in size. Four separate Indian encampments had grown adjacent to the fort. As at Edmonton, the Indians far outnumbered the white population.

Wagons were available to take disembarking passengers across the flats and up the hill to the town. When I asked the teamster where I should begin looking for work, he answered, "You might try Smart's General Store on the main street. You can never tell who you'll run into there. You might get lucky." He wasn't hopeful about my chances of finding anything locally but added that there were a few traders around who might be seeking help. He warned that some were unscrupulous individuals.

Plenty of Indians were moving about the place, scary and pathetic at the same time, like most of the others I'd seen from Gastown to here. There were a half dozen in the store making purchases, an altogether peaceful and disappointing scene that didn't quite fit in with what I had imagined. A couple of white men, who I guessed might be traders, were off to one side, talking. The bespectacled grey-haired man behind the counter ignored the Indians in favour of me and seemed deflated that I was merely inquiring about work and not making a purchase. Like his counterpart in Edmonton, he suggested trying at the fort.

Leaving the store, I hadn't gone far when a voice from behind hailed me and I turned to see one of the men who had been conversing in the store striding toward me. He was perhaps in his mid-20s, a few years older than I. His clean-shaven face was pleasant, with a long nose, a small mouth and wide ears. He dressed in the manner of cowboys, the brim of one side of his Stetson folded up and pinned to the crown, a faded red polka-dot bandana tied around his neck, leather trousers and riding boots. He had a bowie knife in a leather sheath on his belt and carried himself with the assurance of a much older man.

"If you want work, maybe I can help," he said.

While he seemed a very amiable fellow, I remembered the teamster's warning and didn't think it would hurt to be on my guard. I asked, "What have you got?"

He stuck out his hand. "Bill Cameron."

His grip was unusually firm, unintentionally, I thought, because I doubted that he was trying to impress me. Nevertheless, it prompted me to squeeze hard too. "Jack Strong," I said.

"Oh," he said, and I saw the quip forming behind his eyes. I jumped in.

"I'm younger than you thought. Right?"

He threw his head back and laughed. "I'm a trader," he said. "My partner had to go to Winnipeg on family business just as we were about to head out to trade with the Indians west of here. After that, we were going up to Fort Pitt in time for the annuity payments. I could use a hand between here and Pitt. I can't offer you much except grub and 20 per cent of the profits."

I had no idea what annuity payments were and didn't ask because I didn't think much of his offer. Just then, two Indians came out of the store and Cameron excused himself to speak to them. My estimation of him went up several notches when he used their native tongue. I had no way of telling, but he seemed as articulate in what I presumed was Cree as he was in English. And they seemed to like him. All of a sudden, his proposal took on a new dimension. Since things in the territory were apparently peaceful and there was no denying that I needed work, maybe I could learn something from Cameron about the business of trading. Also, if the Indians were potentially my enemy, it wouldn't hurt to know more about them. Cameron seemed trustworthy enough so I put my misgivings aside and after the Indians had left, I said, "It sounds reasonable to me." We shook hands again and agreed to meet at the store first thing in the morning to load the wagon.

Excited over the prospect of going off with Cameron, I was at the store early, worried that he might have changed his mind. But he arrived promptly with a buckboard pulled by two sorrel mares. In behind the wagon seat were a tent and cooking utensils, a spare wheel and two worn saddles and bridles, brought along in the event the wagon broke down beyond repair.

"What about the supplies?" I asked.

"We make a *travois* and travel like the Indians," he said blandly, as if he'd done it dozens of times before.

We loaded our food on the wagon first, up by the saddles where we could easily get at it. The range of the menu was plainly limited. Besides coffee, tea, and sugar, the rest was flour and bacon. Lots of bacon.

"You won't get fat," said Cameron grinning. "Then again, you won't starve either. We can also get fish and dried berries from the Indians. Maybe even a dog roast if you're hungry enough."

The idea of eating dog meat was revolting and seemed to me another indication of the Indians' savage nature.

After loading our supplies, we piled on the trade goods, the bulk of them being blankets, shawls, hats, handkerchiefs, rings and knives. Cameron told me that the Indians on the reserves we'd be visiting had already received their annuities and spent most of it in town.

"But there's always a little left over and since we have to go that way anyway, we might as well try to do some business."

Cameron cleared up his bill at the store. We climbed aboard and with a snap of the reins and a "Giddup!" clattered down the slope to the ferry crossing on the Battle River. After gaining the far side, we headed west into the sun-beaten prairie, along a hard-baked, rutted trail that dipped and rose across open meadows and between stands of poplar. With any luck at all, Cameron reckoned, we would reach the first reserve by dinnertime.

There was little to do but talk, and over the course of the day we learned each other's history. Intelligent and articulate, Cameron had more words at his disposal than most men; he strung them together well, and in a fashion that was never condescending. He was from Trenton, Ontario. After leaving high school, he trained as a pharmacist, learning how to mix prescriptions and sell patent medicines. He claimed he liked the selling part of it the best, for he was gregarious and enjoyed having an ear to bend. He had a cousin who had joined the North-West Mounted Police when they were formed and trekked west with them. Upon his return several years later, he gave Cameron a Sioux arrow that was purportedly stained with Custer's blood. It fired Cameron's imagination enough to bring him west where he learned the trader's art. He had been working in the Fort Battleford area for nearly four years and had got to know the Indians well, and they him. They called him "Nichawamis," a generic, inclusive name which meant "My Little Brother."

Cameron asked about me and I filled him in, even about my father, how he had driven me from home, and the long road that had brought me here from Gastown.

FIVE

The Lesson

CAMERON LENT A SYMPATHETIC ear for the most part but caught me up on the newspaper article that had caused me to come to the prairies.

"You've got the wrong idea, Jack," he said. "You can't blame the Indians for what's happening here. Sure, it's easy to find fault with them, especially when they don't live up to our ideals, but how on earth can they? How can we expect them to learn in a few years what's taken us centuries to learn?"

"But didn't the Indians beat the agent up with an axe handle?"

Cameron shook his head. "They gave him what was more than likely a well-deserved rap on the shoulder. They hurt his feelings more than anything else. I admit that it wasn't the smartest thing in the world to do but the Indian who did it is a bit of a brute. His name is Kahweechetwaymot, which means

'Man Who Speaks Another Tongue,' the other tongue being Blackfoot. I know him well, and I also know Craig, the agent. Between you, me and the gatepost he could stand to learn a few manners too. Anyway, since they didn't understand each other, it boiled down to a lack of communication and there wasn't an interpreter handy. If you want my opinion, I think Craig should have taken the time to learn a little Cree. He's been out here long enough and it might have helped matters. He was the instructor, after all, and it's a job that requires him to deal with the Cree. Maybe if he'd been a bit more diligent, some of the trouble could have been avoided."

I hadn't read a newspaper since I left Gastown so I asked Cameron to tell me the details.

"Well, Craig believed he was above a rap on the arm from an Indian so he went to the police at Battleford. They sent an officer out to arrest Man Who Speaks Another Tongue but by the time he got there the fellow had bragged so much about how he showed a white man who was boss that it got the other warriors excited. It didn't help that they were holding a Thirst Dance at the time—that's how braves are made. The young men skewer the skin on their chests with bone hooks attached to ropes tied to a pole, then dance around it until they're in a trance and the skewers are ripped from their flesh. I've seen them do it and it isn't easy to watch, believe me. Anyway, the officer showed up during this dance and was more or less told that he had a lot of nerve thinking he could arrest anyone, let alone Man Who Speaks Another Tongue, and that he should return to his superior at Battleford and tell him that.

"Superintendent Crozier, the commanding officer, was

indignant to say the least, so he formed a troop and rode out to the reserve. He spoke to Chief Poundmaker—one big chief to another, you know—and demanded that Man Who Speaks Another Tongue be delivered up instantly. You'll meet Poundmaker, or Pitikwahanapiwiyin—that's his Indian name—on this trip, Jack, and you'll see what I mean when I say this is one fine-looking Indian. He has great dignity and presence and he's not about to let anyone tell him what to do. He told Crozier not to be so hasty and insisted that the matter required discussion. 'The sun will not go out,' he said, or words to that effect.

"Crozier had the good sense to agree and much later in the day they reached a compromise. Poundmaker would hand over Man Who Speaks Another Tongue but only if his trial was held on the reserve and not back in Battleford. This was set to happen the next day at noon. But Crozier found the Indians a little too belligerent for his liking and sent word back to the fort for reinforcements. He also had his men empty out the government warehouse that was filled with food, just in case the Indians decided to raid it. This lack of trust angered the band even more, so they surrounded Crozier, whooping and hollering and firing their weapons into the air. The police carried on as if nothing was happening and, luckily, nothing really serious did. It worried Crozier enough, though, that he had his men build a makeshift fort out of three log buildings near the reserve. He strengthened the breastwork with the bags of flour and oats and sides of bacon they had taken from the warehouse. In the morning, reinforcements arrived—60 men and a handful of civilian volunteers."

"Against how many?" I asked.

"Hundreds." He chuckled. "But then men like Crozier believe that odds of ten to one in favour of the Indians make things about even."

Cameron went on to explain that when the time for the trial rolled around, Man Who Speaks Another Tongue didn't show up. Crozier, not a man who liked to have his authority flouted, was beside himself. He went straightaway to see Poundmaker who said his braves had too much pride to give up a fellow warrior. Crozier believed the prestige of the police was at stake and neither man was willing to budge. The superintendent finally gave up in frustration and went back to his makeshift fort.

Poundmaker was afraid that the police were preparing to make war on his people, and went to see Crozier. He offered himself in place of Man Who Speaks Another Tongue but Crozier wouldn't have it. The Chief wanted the real culprit, not a substitute, even if it was a chief. Poundmaker went away to consult with his people but Crozier didn't give them much time. He mustered his men and went and told Poundmaker that he had come for Man Who Speaks Another Tongue and he would not be stopped.

"Remember that dignity I was telling you about, Jack? Well, it disappeared just like that," Cameron said, snapping his fingers. "Poundmaker stamped his foot and said, 'He will not be given up! You say you are going to take him? Take me, if you dare!' He waved his *pukamakin* around—that's a war club with three knives sticking out from the end of it—but he was so frustrated that he ended up cutting his own leg. One of the constables thought Crozier would be next so he pushed the superintendent out of the way and stuck a carbine against Poundmaker's throat. They tell me that the tension was un-be-lievable." Cameron broke the word into three parts to emphasize it. "A slip of that trigger finger and all hell would have broken loose. And just when it seemed things couldn't get any worse, Wandering Spirit stepped in."

We crossed a creek and climbed a long incline to a low ridge and Cameron pulled the wagon to a halt to rest the horses. A hawk wheeled overhead in a restless sky of fleecy clouds that sent dark shadows drifting across the land. The distance in all directions to the horizon was enormous and the light was enough to make an artist weep with joy.

"You'll recognize Wandering Spirit, Jack, if you ever run into him," he continued. He's the only Indian I've ever seen whose hair is in ringlets. Makes a lot of women envious," he said with a small laugh. "I've never believed that one colour of people was any better or any worse than another. Red, yellow, black or white, they're all the same to me. Some of us are decent folk and some aren't, and the colour of a man's skin has nothing to do with it. Wandering Spirit just happens to be one of the bad ones and he'd be a mean son-of-a-bitch in any colour. He has 13 Blackfoot scalps to his credit and never lets anyone forget it."

My eyes widened at the statistic. This was the kind of Indian I had imagined, not the ones who shopped at the Battleford store.

"He's Big Bear's war chief. Now, Big Bear is undoubtedly the most powerful of all the Cree chiefs and he had come to the reserve for the Thirst Dance. But he recognized Poundmaker's authority and kept out of the way. Not Wandering Spirit, though—he wasn't that diplomatic. You see, Jack, Big Bear only has political control over his band. If there's a threat of war, the war chief takes over and that's why Wandering Spirit stuck his nose in."

"What did he do?" I was all ears, utterly captivated by the story.

"He walked up to one of the policemen and stuck the barrel of his rifle in the man's chest and there was a stand-off for a while. I tell you, Jack, if anybody was capable of pulling the trigger it had to be Wandering Spirit, and why he didn't, I'll never know. He's one dangerous human being. Crozier ordered his man to lower his rifle, and Wandering Spirit lowered his, too.

"You might think that Crozier would have let it go at that, but not on your life. The white man's law was being defied and doing nothing about it would be setting a bad precedent. Call him stubborn or stupid but he ordered two of his men to grab Man Who Speaks Another Tongue, who was standing nearby. I don't how they got away with it but they did. Some officers surrounded them and they moved into the temporary fort. The Indians nearly went crazy. But no one fired, which is one of the great mysteries. Maybe they realized that any blood spilled there would just be the beginning."

Cameron snapped the reins and the wagon jerked forward over the rough trail.

"What happened then?" I asked.

"It was Angus McKay who defused the situation. McKay is

the local Company man and the Indians have great respect for him. They've named him Little Bear. He suggested distracting the Indians by giving them all the flour, oats and bacon the police had used as a part of the fort's breastwork. Crozier was opposed to the idea at first but then saw the wisdom in it. The Indians were more hungry than they were angry and the ploy worked. While they were grabbing the food, Crozier spirited Man Who Speaks Another Tongue off to Fort Battleford and that was pretty much the end of things."

"What happened to him?"

"He spent a week in jail and Poundmaker was pleased because he was afraid Kahweechetwaymot would be hanged. Craig was given a well-deserved dressing-down by his superiors." Cameron sighed. "We came close to an all-out war though, Jack, and the situation hasn't improved much. God knows what the outcome will be but one thing's certain—a belly rumbling from hunger doesn't care much about keeping the peace. The government promised to supply the Cree with food while they converted to reserve life and learned how to farm. The Indian agents are responsible for doling it out but a lot of them act as if they paid for the food out of their own bloody pockets. They won't give it out unless they think the Indians are earning it through hard work."

We trundled along through the patchy sunlight, the wagon a schoolhouse and Cameron the teacher. Spurts of dust from the wheels were picked up by the wind and sent spiralling off behind us. We stopped for lunch in the shade of some poplars before continuing on to the first reserve. The wind began to build in the afternoon heat and the makings of thunderclouds sat on the horizon. Cameron told me more about the Cree.

He said that they were divided into two large tribes: the Plains Cree whose traditional hunting grounds were south of the North Saskatchewan River, and the Woods Cree who hunted north of it. He didn't know their numbers but reckoned it couldn't be more than 10 thousand, with the Plains Cree in the majority. These two large groups were split into smaller ones, such as the River People and the Prairie People, who lived and traded in specific areas and who in turn were split into bands, each led by a chief.

"A chief gets to be a chief only if he deserves it," Cameron went on. "Most of them are charismatic and intelligent men who are able to inspire and lead people. Typically there'll be about a hundred or so followers, but chiefs like Poundmaker and Big Bear attract many more."

He shook the reins and urged the horses up another low ridge.

"The Indians we'll be trading with are the River People, and the reserves they live on are named after the chiefs. The first one is Sweet Grass, then comes Poundmaker and Little Pine—they've joined together. When we get to Sweet Grass, Jack, you just smile a lot and show the people you're friendly. I have a few beads you can hand out, and that ought to put you in their good books. Keep in mind that you can only be one of two things to these people—a friend or an enemy. Being a friend is wisest."

A marker post sunk into the ground beside the trail was the only indication that we had entered the reserve. Later, we passed small fields of grain and corn and smaller plots of

other vegetables that were well tended. No one was out working in the hot sun. I mentioned to Cameron how neat and
productive the fields appeared.

"These are better than most, Jack, and it's probably
because the women here look after them. On some reserves
no one does the work. You'd think it would be the men doing
it but they don't operate the way we do. We expect our people
to put in a full day's work but the only time they ever did that
was when they built their buffalo pounds. Now the buffalo are
gone and they haven't adapted to planting crops. It's all happened so fast they haven't had time to get used to the idea.
There's not much for them to be happy about and when you
add hunger to the list, well . . ." He let the thought trail off.

Alongside a clear creek was an encampment of many skin
lodges and two rough-hewn log buildings. Horses grazed in a
fenced-off area nearby and several wagons and carts sat side by
side beyond the lodges. The men and women were awaiting
us, made aware of our pending arrival through the moccasin
telegraph, which Cameron said was more effective out here
than the wire variety. They gathered around us like children
around a Christmas tree, led by an older man with a heavily
furrowed face who was partially dressed in white men's clothes.
There were cries of "*Ta'nisi*," to which Cameron replied,
"*M'on~ana'ntaw. Ki'n~a ma'ka?*"

He turned to me. "They're just asking how we're doing."

There were plenty of smiles for Cameron as we got down
from the wagon and I heard his Indian name used several
times. We were invited to set up our own tent beyond the
lodges, and then Cameron got down to the business of

trading. I watched and smiled and could see that many of the Indians were driving hard bargains. We ended up with a bit more cash than when we arrived, but mostly we acquired animal skins: coyote, deer and muskrat. Cameron told me, "Some of them have money and others have skins, which are as valuable as money because we can sell them to the Company at Fort Pitt. This is the way it always is unless you catch them on payday."

"Which one is Sweet Grass?" I asked Cameron, although I presumed he was the older man in the partial suit.

"Sweet Grass died a long time ago." He nodded toward the person I'd picked out. "Strike Him On The Back is chief now."

"Why is he the only one wearing white man's clothes?"

"The treaty Sweet Grass signed entitles him to a new suit every three years."

I gave the few beads I had to a pretty girl about my age, which caused a stir of laughter among those who saw it. She smiled at me and said, "*Kinana'skomitin,*" which I would soon learn meant "Thank you." Afterward, Cameron said that the Indians had appreciated the gesture and had referred to me as "Crooked Tooth." While the name didn't quite measure up to "Jack Strong," like all Indian names it was perfectly apt: the last incisor on the right side of my mouth was set back from the others and was quite noticeable when I smiled.

After the trading, the band invited us to join them for some feasting, singing and dancing in our honour. The food wasn't much different from what Cameron and I had been eating. There was jackfish, full of bones and lacking flavour, and though it seemed in short supply, we appeared to get the lion's share. Cameron said that the feast would mean that our hosts wouldn't be eating as well the next day, but it was important for them to be generous.

In the evening everyone formed into a large circle and the dancing and singing began. I couldn't make anything of it and Cameron was so mesmerized by it all I didn't ask him to explain. During a pause, the girl I had given the beads to came over and handed me a small, worn, but beautifully beaded pouch. She pointed to herself and said, "*Kees-ka-na-kwas,*" then, pointing to the pouch, "*O-ska-yi.*"

I looked at Cameron. "Her name is Kees-ka-na-kwas, which means 'Cut Sleeve,' and she says the gift is new."

But it clearly wasn't and I said so.

"It's new to you," Cameron said. "That's what she means. It's a gift that's new to you and you're expected to get up and dance to show your appreciation." He grinned at the prospect.

Dance? I had tried to avoid it all of my life and would have been perfectly happy to keep it that way. Over in the west the thunderclouds that had been building since the late afternoon released a far-off rolling boom. I wished it would rain. I hesitated, not knowing what to do. I turned to Cameron.

"Go for it, Jack," he said. "Tonight they're dancing for pleasure, so just get up and move your feet around like they do. They'll be honoured by the gesture. No need to do anything fancy—the point is to have fun."

Well, I knew something about having fun, so I tied the pouch to my belt, got to my feet and began shuffling in time to the beat of the drum, circling the fire in the centre. At first

I wished I had a partner, as I felt awkward and conspicuous, but since none of the other dancers seemed to be paying me any attention I warmed to the task. When Cameron himself got up and joined in, I let myself get lost in it. It was dancing that demanded little and gave much in terms of freedom.

The festivities continued until the western sky had become a menacing black monster spitting streaks of lightning and farting thunder. A cool wind gusted through the camp and people ran for their lodges. Cameron and I hastily threw a tarp over our wagon and were tying it down just as the storm exploded around us. Rain fell as if the bottom had dropped out of a lake and we were near soaked by the time we reached the refuge of our tent.

The thunderstorm lasted for more than a half-hour and by then it was too late to resume dancing. The camp remained relatively quiet, except for the sound of voices in conversation and prowling dogs that barked occasionally. We prepared for bed by the light of a candle in a holder attached to the centre pole of the tent. My mind was awhirl with all the information Cameron had given me and with the events of the day, especially the evening we had spent with these strange people. I had left Gastown spoiling for a fight, never dreaming that I'd be breaking bread with the very enemy I had come to wage war against. It evoked feelings that I didn't understand and it made me restless. There are few things as unsettling as having your illusions shattered.

Cameron must have sensed my mood. He said, "You'd better try and get some rest, Jack. We've another long day ahead of us tomorrow."

I had too many questions running through my mind to sleep. The people I had met that day were different from me and yet in many ways they weren't. I was bewildered and said as much to Cameron.

He didn't respond right away; instead, he reached for his coat and took a box of wooden matches from an inside pocket. It had a picture of a bird on the top and some writing on the bottom. He held it up between us so that I could see only the writing. "What do you see, Jack?" he asked.

I was a little confused. "I see a small box with writing on it."

"That's odd. I see a small box with a picture of a bird on it."

"Turn it around and look at the side I'm seeing."

"That's easy enough to do with a box of matches but what if it was the world and the way people live that we were looking at? Think of the significance of that, Jack. You see it one way and I see it another and your point of view depends entirely on where you sit. You can describe to me in detail what your side looks like but I'll never see it quite the way you do, never truly understand it. That's the way it is with Indians and white people. And if you want to call yourself 'civilized,' then the onus is on you to remember that we see things differently. You'll never make it as a trader if you don't and if you do, dealing with them will be a lot more enjoyable and a lot less frustrating."

I went to bed with the image of the matchbox flitting around in my mind like a small bird, trying to apply it to some of the things I'd seen and some of the things Cameron had told me about the Indians. It was an abstract idea with practical applications and made perfect sense to me. And I could see that while I had always considered Indians more savage than white men, I now understood why they would think the same about us. When I expressed this to Cameron he said that the Indians did indeed think we were savages, particularly in the way we treat the children of parents who had died. We put them in an orphanage and paid someone to care for them but among the Indians, children belonged to all the people and never wanted for love or a home if their parents died.

I had picked up a few handy Cree words during the transactions and the evening's dancing and I tossed them around in my mind until I knew them almost as well as my own name. *Ta'nisi, kinana'skomitin,* and especially Kees-ka-na-kwas, which slipped off the tongue like a song.

Come morning the skies had cleared and the air was cooler. Though the camp never seemed to quiet down completely, it came instantly alive as Cameron and I arose and prepared breakfast. We shared one of our sides of bacon with the band, then struck the tent, still damp from the storm, and laid it out flat in the back of the wagon to dry. We bade farewell to Strike Him On The Back and his people and, after crossing the creek, set out for Poundmaker's reserve. I felt buoyant, as if I had passed from a dark room into one with a brightly burning lamp. I was ready to face anything the day might bring.

When we arrived at Poundmaker's, Cameron pointed out the place where the police had built their temporary fort. The poplar logs that formed part of the breastwork were still in place next to the small building, as if there might be a use for them again. We saw no agriculture here. Cameron said that while we would probably find both Poundmaker and Little Pine on their reserves, neither chief had quite come to terms with the settled life imposed upon them and still liked to roam from time to time.

We passed the location of the Thirst Dance held back in June during the time of the troubles. Though deserted now, the area was well trampled. Cameron estimated that there had been more than a hundred lodges on the site at the time; Indians had come from all around.

Cameron didn't formally introduce me to Poundmaker but I saw him close up and can tell you that he was a magnificent specimen of a man. Named after his father, who had also made the best buffalo pounds in the territory, he was the spitting image of the Indians I'd seen in drawings in those dime western novels, with high, prominent cheekbones separated by a classic Roman nose, as handsome a man as you'd find anywhere. He wore his hair in a single long braid that reached to his buttocks, tied with a red bandana and decorated with mink skin. Unlike Strike Him On The Back, he did not wear white men's clothing and had on instead full Indian regalia, his leather vest studded with the heads of brass nails. He was definitely a man fully aware that his place in life was at the top of the heap—any heap, Indian or white. He didn't need to speak to command anyone's respect but people listened when he did.

Poundmaker and his people weren't as happy to see us as were Strike Him On The Back's people at Sweet Grass. He was still bearing a grudge from the events in June and although he and his band took what advantage they could of our trade goods, we didn't feel welcome enough to linger so we moved on to Little Pine. It was just a few miles up the road and we received pretty much the same reception. Nevertheless, we sold most of our goods and left a side of bacon, as we had at Poundmaker's.

A few miles beyond the encampment, we forded the Battle River in water up to our wheel hubs. Though we saw no markers, once we assumed we were well past the boundaries of the reserve, we stopped for the night. It was almost dusk as we set up camp behind a copse of poplars, out of sight of anyone travelling on the road. Cameron didn't think we had anything to worry about, but he said, "There are rogues in every walk and way of life and the Indians are no different from anyone else. You'd do well to remember that, Jack. It's always better to be safe than sorry, at least that's my take on it. In fact, that was another reason why I hired you to come along. It wasn't so much that I needed a hand as it was recognizing that it's always safer to ride in pairs out here."

We spent a quiet night, the prairie silent and still as a pond, rippled only by the crackling fire and Cameron's violin. He was an avid player and always carried his instrument under the seat of the wagon on trading junkets. Though I was no judge in the matter, the few slow airs he played seemed quite accomplished. I hadn't much experience listening to a violin and there was a touch of melancholia to it that made me think of home. I wondered what Ma would have thought had she been able to see me these past couple of days. I don't suppose she would have been happy about it.

During breakfast the next morning, we heard the drum-beat of hooves and the squeak of wagon wheels approaching. It was a small group of Indians heading in the direction of Little Pine. Cameron showed himself, extended his arm with his hand open, and gave them the traditional salute. A couple of them saluted back but the party didn't stop and disappeared quickly over the first rise of land. We struck camp and set out for Fort Pitt, some 60 or 70 miles to the northwest, and much of the journey was filled with Cameron's descriptions of treaties and reserves, and their impact on the Cree.

The treaty that the Cree had signed was Treaty Six and with it, they surrendered all of the land around the North Saskatchewan River, more than 120,000 square miles. In exchange, they got reserves that amounted to a section of land, or one square mile, for each family of five. "You only need basic arithmetic to see that 5 divided into 10,000, the approximate Cree population, comes out to 2,000 square miles. It isn't much when you think of it. But, you know, I'm not sure they knew that they were signing the land away. They knew that the treaty meant reserves, but they have no concept of land ownership, so how could they sign away something they didn't feel they owned?"

In addition to the land, each chief or headman received a $25 annuity, each councillor $15, each man, woman and child $5. The chief also got a horse and wagon upon signing and a new set of clothes every three years. The band got agricultural tools, livestock and an instructor to teach them how to farm. Included was a clause stipulating that the government would provide them with food should they suffer pestilence or famine. "As far as the Indians are concerned," Cameron said, "they've been in a state of famine ever since the buffalo disappeared, and they think that the government ought to provide them with food until their farms can sustain them. So they see the government's refusal to co-operate as a broken promise. It's a sore spot among the Indians, Jack, and any small thing that comes along, such as the Man Who Speaks Another Tongue incident, is like a hard kick on a bruised shin."

Cameron spoke of how Big Bear was one of the first to oppose the treaty. "He was relatively unknown until then but many of the Cree liked what he had to say, and that elevated his status. He's a powerful orator and he thought he could broker a better deal with the whites, but he never reckoned he'd be up against a whole battery of shrewd lawyers. He's a peaceful man, though, and he encouraged his people not to take up arms against the whites. I suppose he was also wise enough to know that they would lose if they did. In the end, he gave in and signed but he wouldn't accept a reserve. To him they were prisons and he wanted no part of them, unlike the Woods Cree, by the way. They settled into their reserves more readily because it didn't change their lifestyle that much. They're hunters and trappers and they've traded with the Company for nearly as long as it's been here. They still do. But if you've been following the buffalo for generations, it's a hard thing to leave behind. Big Bear's a nomad. It's what he's done all his life, just like his forefathers, and he refuses to live any other way. That was the main reason why, besides the Thirst Dance, Big Bear was on Poundmaker's reserve when the trouble started. He was seeking his friend's support. Now he's up with the Woods Cree at Frog Lake, but you'll see him at Fort Pitt when he comes down for his pay."

In three days, we were back on the high benches of the North Saskatchewan. The river flowed peaceably below, reflecting the deep blue of the sky; on the opposite bank sat Fort Pitt. I had been there less than two weeks ago when we dropped off mail from Edmonton and picked up more passengers, yet it seemed like years. We bounced down the terraced slope to catch the Company scow that would take us across the river.

We had a few weeks to wait for Cameron's partner, George Dill. On his return from Winnipeg, he would be stopping in Battleford to purchase new supplies to sell to the Indians when they came to Fort Pitt in October for their annuity payments. Cameron said that after the annuities, he and Dill planned on building a store in the settlement at Frog Lake. Big Bear and his sizeable band were camped there, plus some Woods Cree on their reserve, so business ought to be good. "But knowing the Indians," he added, "they'll buy everything George brings with him on this trip and that'll mean returning to Battleford for more supplies. It'll also mean that I could use your help building the store, if you're interested."

I had a vague idea where Frog Lake was for I remembered the steamer stopping at a place called Frog Creek Landing, and I presumed the creek connected the lake to the river. I also knew that Cameron was a man of his word. He had paid me faithfully and he was trustworthy and reliable, as well as a useful man to have around when there were Indians in the vicinity. Besides, I had enjoyed the trip up from Battleford more than anything I had previously experienced, not only for the sheer adventure of it but for the pleasure of Cameron's informative and amiable company. Over the miles, I had made a valued friend and that was no mean thing in this lonely country. I accepted his offer.

SIX

Fort Pitt

FORT PITT WAS NO FORT AT ALL, merely a collection of six Hudson's Bay Company buildings in a square between the river and a low ridge, with outbuildings and a large corral for livestock, all surrounded by grass trampled and chewed to stubble by grazing cattle. It housed several Company employees under the eagle eye of the factor, William McLean, and a handful of North-West Mounted Police under the red-streaked eyes of Inspector Francis Dickens.

I had never met a man like Dickens. He was short and balding with a long, reddish beard and a perpetually sullen face. He was the runt of the litter born to the novelist Charles Dickens and his wife and, like other short men I'd met, compensated for his lack of height with cockiness. His family was friendly with Lord Dufferin, Canada's Governor General, who got Dickens his commission in the NWMP. He hadn't a single qualification for the job; the objective was to get him out of England to a place where he wouldn't be a bother to his family. Recognizing his incompetence, his superiors kept him in the east until there was such a shortage of officers in the North-West Territories that they reluctantly sent him to Blackfoot Crossing, near Calgary. There, on three occasions, his tactlessness nearly led to war with the Blackfoot. He was then assigned to Fort Pitt so that Superintendent Crozier, in Fort Battleford, could keep tabs on him. Dickens stuttered when he spoke and was partially deaf, but refused to admit it. Rather than walk he strutted, his chest thrust exaggeratedly forward. In his days of confiscating illegal liquor from the whisky traders in the area, he must have kept a little for himself, for he was a chronic alcoholic. Behind his back, he was called "Chickenstalker," a nickname given him by his father that had somehow found its way to the Canadian west.

Cameron and I had time to spare while we waited for the arrival of Dill and the Indians, so when I admitted that I'd never ridden a horse, he insisted that I begin to learn that very instant. We saddled up the sorrel mares he used to pull the wagon and rode off into the surrounding countryside, walking at first, then speeding up a little, as I learned to use the reins and my legs to give the horse commands. I juddered along with my teeth rattling in my head until Cameron told me to move with the horse, not against it.

"Relaxing is the key," he said. "Sit up straight and deep in the saddle, and keep your feet forward. *Feel* the rhythm of the animal."

Once I grasped this concept, I heeled my mount into a full gallop. Cameron was right. I began to feel as though I had achieved a connection with it. We came back over the ridge at a fast pace and things were going so well I thought I might as well continue past the entrance to the corral, and show off my riding prowess to the men working nearby. However, Cameron had neglected to tell me that horses have a keenly developed and unerring sense of direction back to the stable, and will go there with little or no prodding. In mid-stride, it seemed, the horse did an abrupt left turn into the corral. It was so sudden that I failed to go with it and went flying off at an angle into a small pile of manure. I was stunned that it had happened so fast, yet not so stunned that I couldn't hear the uproarious laughter from those watching. The horse was waiting placidly at the entrance to the stable as I crawled sheepishly from the pile. One of the least offensive of animal excrements, horse manure has an almost sweet smell to it. But not when it's up your nose.

"The bathtub's that way," someone joked, pointing to the swirling river just 150 yards away.

I took the hint.

I was the talk of the fort for a couple of days but I kept on riding; I even practised taking the horse across the river, letting it do all the work while I hung onto its tail. It was an efficient way to have a bath and wash your clothes at the same time.

Cameron owned a shotgun and a rifle and offered to teach me how to use them. All I had to do was pay for the ammunition, which I did gladly. We went beyond the ridge and set up stationary targets of empty tin cans. Moving targets were jack rabbits and prairie dogs, and for the shotgun, prairie chickens and grouse. They were hard to hit but I got so I was a reasonably good shot, even from the back of a horse. Yet I wondered how Wild Jack Strong had managed to shoot as well as he did at a full gallop.

When I asked him about revolvers, Cameron said that he had never fired one and didn't know how they compared to rifles and shotguns. But he had heard of a shoot-out down in Montana where the two antagonists clasped left hands and fired away at each other point blank. Several shots missed and a few hit, although none fatally.

"Those old bullets contained low-velocity gunpowder, so the slug would often enter a man and not go in very deep. I've met men carrying up to a half-dozen in their hide."

Cameron put names to birds for me, such as the whip-poor-will and passenger pigeon, and pointed out the plants I should know about: saskatoon berries, chokecherries, cranberries and hazelnuts, and many others that provided sustenance. He made me aware of the sky, teaching me the constellations, about the North Star, and the phases of the moon, which he called the "Indians' calendar." He taught me more Cree, too, mostly words rather than how to string them together, but that would come in time. He reckoned a winter among the Cree at Frog Lake would do the trick.

We went on in this vein almost daily because he felt knowledge was fundamental to survival in this country. He didn't have all the answers by a long shot but he liked that I asked so many questions. It was a new world for me and I was eager to participate in it, to absorb as much of it as I could.

I was beginning to love the prairie, its rolling expanse and endless sky, and when I thought of the coast, it seemed close and stifling.

I had time to sit down and write to Joe and did so. It had only been a matter of weeks since I'd last seen him but so much had been packed into that span of time it felt like months. I wrote down every detail of my new life and then I wrote Ma but I did not tell her half of what I told Joe.

And so we waited for the Indians to arrive for their annuity payments and for George Dill to arrive with the goods for them to spend it on. There was no shortage of things to do around the fort. Something always wanted mending, the animals needed tending to, and Cameron and I spent many an hour in the poplars beyond the ridge cutting and hauling firewood. In such ways we earned our bed and board. It was not an unpleasant routine and there was a great camaraderie among everyone as the fort was prepared for winter.

Most evenings were spent in the reception hall, chatting, playing parlour games or cards, or simply listening to McLean's daughters perform. McLean had nine children and the three oldest were girls—Amelia, Eliza and Kitty. They filled what would normally have been a quiet place with bustle and chatter, all those feminine things that drive some men to distraction and nourish others. To keep them occupied, their father had bought an organ, a fiddle and a banjo, and I would often hear the girls practising. They were quite accomplished and they could sing, too, with voices that carried a song straight to the heart. I enjoyed them most when Amelia sang the lead. Her sisters' voices were a bit on the thin side, but hers was quite mature and textured. She sang a musical version of Longfellow's poem *The Bridge* that I particularly liked.

At 16 or 17, Amelia was the oldest. She was full-figured and her jet-black hair complimented an almost pretty face that showed traces of her Indian heritage. Her mother, Helen, was Métis, but I don't think Amelia ever considered herself to be anything other than a human being. She was quick-witted, bright and very talented. Besides playing the organ and singing, she sewed her own dresses, wrote poetry and could make herself understood in Cree as well as English and French.

I slowly got to know her during those evenings in the reception hall. Besides music, Amelia loved to play cribbage and checkers, and would take on all comers. I knew the game of cribbage, having spent many an evening playing it with Ma, and made a worthy opponent for her. There is as much in the luck of the draw as there is skill to the game and, as I had always been lucky at cards, I often beat her handily. Checkers was a different matter. I had played the game with friends and thought at first that I would be nice and let her beat me, but soon discovered that she didn't need my help. She was always thinking several moves ahead and the best I could do was provide her with a reasonable challenge.

No man likes to be beaten, of course, especially by the gentler sex, but despite Amelia's competitiveness, it was her femininity and poise that attracted me. I was grateful for her company and I sensed that she appreciated mine as well. She loved to talk and found in me someone who would listen. Once, our hands touched while she was cutting the cards and the softness of her skin sent an unexpected thrill through me. If she felt anything she cleverly hid it.

THE DAYS were getting shorter; the nights were colder and in the mornings, the land wore a thin veil of frost. Ice, like a delicate lace, was forming around the edges of ponds. The leaves of the poplar trees along the ridge above the fort and in the coulees had turned yellow and in some cases disappeared altogether. The mosquitoes and flies were gone till spring and that was a blessing.

One night, over cards, Amelia said that she and her sisters were going up on the ridge the coming Sunday for a picnic and I was welcome to join them if I wished. She had asked her father and he had approved. I didn't like the idea of her sisters tagging along and hoped that there might be a chance that Amelia and I could wander off on our own. I said that I would love to go. But the next day Big Bear and his band arrived and set up camp behind the ridge. They were in a sour mood so McLean recommended that the girls not stray too far from the fort.

George Dill arrived with the trade goods. It was clear by the warmth of their handshake that he and Cameron held each other in high regard. An intense man, Dill was in his late 30s or early 40s. He had a goatee that was kept well trimmed, and a wave of hair that jutted up like a ship's prow from his high forehead when the wind didn't have its way with it. He was married with two children but was not going to bring his family out from Bracebridge, Ontario, until he had established himself in the Territories. He thanked me for helping Bill and appreciated that I planned to go up to Frog Lake after the annuities to help build their store; he assured me I would be well paid.

The annuity payments could not commence until the Indian agent arrived with the money. He rode in with a police escort in mid-October. Thomas Quinn was an arrogant individual, typical of many agents who thought they were doing the Indians a big favour by giving them the money that was theirs in the first place. Big Bear and his people knew him well, and they had little liking for him. He had a commanding presence, standing nearly six and a half feet tall, with a thick, drooping moustache that helped disguise a chin too narrow for his upper face. If you didn't recognize him by his height, you could pick him out by the Scottish tam that he always wore, an unusual hat for this country. The Indians called him Kapwatamut, meaning "Sioux Speaker." Quinn not only spoke the language but had a small quantity of Sioux blood flowing through his veins. Yet as a teenager during the wars in Minnesota, he had fought against the Sioux, and had also served in the American Civil War. Well educated and intelligent, he was obstinate and uncompromising with the Indians, just the kind of man the government wanted, and they had put him in charge of the Fort Pitt area. Immediately upon his arrival, he sent word out to Big Bear's camp that he was prepared to make the payments on the following day at 9:00 A.M., at the fort, not at the camp.

The morning dawned cold and cloudy. I had just finished tending to the horses when the Indians appeared on the ridge and began descending the gentle slope to the fort. I hurried to the main building, where I knew they were headed, and encountered Cameron, who would act as one of the interpreters for the meeting. He knew there was something in the air and insisted that I should not miss the proceedings. Whatever I didn't understand he would explain to me later.

I stood outside the office while Cameron entered. The Indians filed in and filled the office, then overflowed into the hall. Some had to stand on the stairs leading to the second floor. I was able to hold my position by the door because they didn't crowd me, maybe because they couldn't stand my smell. Outside, they gathered around the office windows and plugged the square in front of the building. They were annoyed and they were painted and armed. Most tried to hide their rifles beneath their blankets but what they were carrying was obvious to anyone with eyes.

I listened intently. None of the Indians spoke English but between the interpreters and what I learned later from Cameron, I was able to piece together the dialogue of the meeting.

At the front of the crowd in the office was Big Bear, his face as creased as a dried fig. Beside him was Wandering Spirit, identifiable by his ringlets. Next to him was Little Poplar, a nephew of Big Bear's who had come from south of the international boundary. He wore a Stetson hat decorated with five feathers and he carried a large bowie knife and two revolvers in his belt. He spoke first.

"I have heard that my people here are hungry and I can see that it is true. I have come to speak for them. I am from below the Medicine Line where the Americans treat their Indians much better. They give them more food and clothing. That is all I will say for now. I will hear what others have to say."

Quinn said nothing, as if Little Poplar had not spoken at all. Then Wandering Spirit spoke up. Cameron's description of him had been spot on. He had a silky, smooth voice.

"We had a friend once, the buffalo, and now that friend is gone. We are destitute when once food was abundant in our world."

There were cries of agreement from others. Little Poplar spoke again, leaning in close to Quinn.

"Are you Sioux Speaker?"

Quinn never flinched. "I am called that."

Sneeringly polite, Little Poplar asked, "May I look at you?"

Quinn stood up, towering over the Indian. He raised his arms and turned once around, clearly enjoying himself. "Have you seen enough?"

A scowl crossed Little Poplar's face. "I know of you," he said. "They speak your name as far away as the Missouri River. They say it is your job to say 'no' to the Indians."

Again, Quinn said nothing. Big Bear, who had been quietly observing, now spoke up, the timbre of his voice as pleasing to the ear as fine music. He glared at Quinn. "I will ask you something, and I will say it only three times before I am finished. You have long ago sent the buffalo away and my people are hungry. Will you kill an ox for us before we are paid?"

"No," Quinn answered adamantly, shaking his head for emphasis. "The cattle the government gives you are for work and milk, not for food."

Technically Quinn was right, but that he would have nothing to do with Big Bear's proposition was a mark of his obstinacy. It was his way or no way.

Little Poplar's accusation of Quinn's purpose confirmed, Big Bear paused, thinking. Then he spoke again.

"When I came from the south, from Little Poplar's territory, I found the ground torn up by two iron lines that stretched away to the east and west. This, I knew, was the iron road, which surely must have been built to bring food and clothing to hungry Indians. I want the big wagons that use the iron road filled with money to be thrown out on both sides so that my people will have plenty of it, and plenty of food. Now I will ask you for the second time, will you kill an ox for us?"

"I've already answered that question," Quinn said, unswayed.

Big Bear turned to the others. "I will have this man removed from here and replaced by a new man before the moon grows old again." He turned back to face Quinn. "I will ask you for the last time, and I want you to answer so that you will be heard by every Indian in this house." He spaced the words out. "Will you give us an ox?"

Quinn, who seemed amused by the exchange, boomed out, "No! I will not say it again."

Big Bear turned to the others and raised his arms. "You have heard him speak. Let him keep the treaty money. Go!"

The Indians nearly trampled over each other heading for the door and getting out of the building. I stayed out of their way, pressed up against the wall. They stomped up the slope and disappeared over the ridge to their encampment. Many had their rifles out and were firing into the air. Shortly afterward, we heard the unsettling mutter of drums.

The incident left me shaken, and alarm spread among the fort's occupants. William McLean was angry and called for a meeting in his office. Quinn and Dickens were there as well as several others. Cameron and I also attended. Concern was etched on everyone's face.

"Good God, man," the factor said to Quinn. "Is it not possible for the government to give them a single ox?"

"It might be possible," said Quinn, ruffled that his authority was under fire. "But not likely while I'm in charge. Rules are rules and we would get nowhere with the Indians without them."

"Even if they understood the language, those kinds of rules mean little, Mr. Quinn. Where do you think that leaves them?"

"They'll learn. They'll have to."

"Your rules are doing more harm than you know," said the factor, bleakly.

Quinn would not be budged. "They get their oxen only when they sign their Xs and settle on their reserves. Big Bear has refused to settle and he will not get his animals until he does."

Other voices spoke out, mostly in support of McLean. Dickens, however, declared that to give the Indians an inch was to give them a mile, that, like children, it was best to be firm right from the start. McLean was about to reply when someone called for silence. Big Bear and one of his sub-chiefs, Miserable Man, were coming to the door.

The two Indians swept into the hallway and into the office, nearly bowling me over. I doubt they even saw me, so great was their focus on their purpose for being there. Big Bear exuded great dignity, Miserable Man contempt. Ignoring Quinn, the Bear walked up to McLean and apologized for his threatening words, adding, "You are a man made to be a chief. Your heart is good and you are our friend. The Hudson's Bay Company has always been a generous friend. This man," he sneered at Quinn, "has a heart of stone." He placed his hands on the side of his head then flung them toward the agent. "Here," he hissed. "If you want my head, take it!"

Miserable Man had a brutish, pockmarked face contorted with anger and his voice was all snarl; he was one of several Indians who wore a scalp-lock. This was a handful of hair tied off at the crown as a sign of bravery, for it dared an enemy to scalp him. Some wore them plaited with strips of fur, as did Miserable Man, who leaned into Quinn and said, "If I need food this winter and you don't give it to me . . ."

He left the threat hanging in the air.

Having said what they had come to say, the two Indians left. Quinn broke the silence.

"If they don't come to terms they won't be paid."

"This is nonsense," said McLean, unable to disguise his anger. He turned to one of his subordinates. "Slaughter one of our oxen and take it to them."

But the gift only partially mollified the Indians. Their issues were not with the Hudson's Bay Company but with the government. Was not the beef supposed to come from it and not from the Company? Nevertheless, they could not reject the thoughtful offer and accepted the meat. They continued to drum and dance, which put the police and every man with a gun on full alert.

Cameron was not in the least threatened by the Indians and instructed me not to worry as he, Dill and I set up the wagon of goods near the encampment. "I wouldn't do this if my name were Quinn," he said. "But they have nothing against you and me and they'll want what we have in the wagon." Indeed, the Indians came and examined everything, coveting each item, despite having no money or furs with which to barter. At all times they were civil, if not friendly, toward us.

After several meetings with his councillors, Big Bear sent word of a compromise. He would accept payment, but only at his encampment, not at the fort. At first Quinn would play no part in it but eventually he succumbed to pressure from McLean and nearly everyone else.

At 8:30 the following morning the agent set up a pay table at the edge of the Indian encampment and waited for them to come to him. People moved about among the lodges but there was no sign of Big Bear. Nine o'clock passed, then 9:30 and still no one came. Quinn was agitated. Having argued against being there in the first place he was now being kept waiting, and he didn't like it. He pulled out his pocket watch and flipped open the top.

"If they are not here by 10:00 they will not get paid."

Quinn left his watch open on the table and we waited. It was as if we were invisible. Right on the dot of 10:00, he shut the lid, pocketed the watch, gathered up the wax-sealed box containing $7,000 of treaty money and, without a word, strode off. He had not quite reached the crest of the ridge when Big Bear, Wandering Spirit and a few other chiefs came from their lodges and hurried over, wanting to know why Quinn was leaving.

"He got tired of waiting," Cameron said.

The Indians were anxious and called after the agent. Quinn turned and stopped, and seemed to be debating with himself as to whether or not he should return. I was anxious and so was Cameron. If Quinn walked away anything could happen, from a deadly battle to Cameron and Dill losing their investment. But he came back down the hill, took his place at the table, opened the box and pulled out enough money for the first payment to Big Bear. Everyone breathed a sigh of relief.

The next two days brought a frenzy of business as the Indians bought up everything we had, as well as goods from another trader. I believe we could have sold a second wagon-load had Dill brought one.

At night we sat and watched them dance and listened to the warriors count *coups*. These were conspicuous acts of bravery that ranged from simply touching an enemy and getting away safely, to killing him, all spoken as statements of fact rather than boasts. Every now and then one of them would point a rifle at Cameron, Dill or me, as if we were the enemy. This worried Cameron: not so much the act of having a gun pointed at us, but more the state of mind of the Indians that would make them do it. The apparent happiness of the celebration was merely a façade that hid something sinister, of that he was certain.

Big Bear and his people packed up and returned to Frog Lake. They left an uneasy feeling in their wake and many at the fort were glad to see the backs of them. Still fresh in everyone's minds was the incident involving Man Who Speaks Another Tongue and the faceoff the previous June between Poundmaker and Crozier. Quinn's stubbornness could have resulted in a similar incident, only with worse consequences. I was beginning to think that if all of the government's Indian agents were like Quinn and Craig, it was a wonder that war hadn't broken out a long time ago.

Cameron and I packed up, too, while Dill left for Battleford to get more supplies. Despite the tension in the fort I was eager to get to Frog Lake. I was lucky to have stumbled into Cameron and I wondered where I'd be if I hadn't. In him I had found a mentor, a knowledgeable, reliable man who had the confidence of all he met, especially the Indians. With him around, I had no qualms about living next to them.

Amelia knew that with Big Bear's departure I would be leaving too. We had not had the opportunity for a picnic, nor to meet alone, and I was pleased that she cared enough to ask if I would be coming back for Christmas.

"Am I invited?" I asked.

"Everyone in the area is invited. I do hope you'll come."

"I will try," I said. But the truth was, I didn't know where I'd be at Christmas.

Cameron and I bought the tools we would need to build the store, loaded them on the wagon with our other supplies and bade everyone goodbye. McLean also said that he hoped to see us at Christmas. Cameron turned over the reins to me and the sorrels needed only a jiggle to get them moving. I drove onto the track leading north and gave the horses their heads. We waved to those who had gathered to see us off and disappeared over the ridge, clattering past Big Bear's trampled encampment, and on into the rolling, tree-crusted, pond-dotted countryside, first to a small post at Onion Lake, then on to Frog Lake several miles beyond.

SEVEN

Frog Lake

IMMEDIATELY UPON OUR ARRIVAL at Frog Lake, Cameron and I set to work building the store, the back of which would serve as our lodging. There was an abundance of straight spruce trees in the area and we felled them for logs, using the horses to drag them to the site. We hired Indians to help us lift the logs into place, then chinked them with mud and straw. It was hard labour and I was stiff and sore at first, but I began to put on muscle with every swing of the axe and hammer. Winter slid down from the north and brought with it the first snow, small, stinging pellets that swirled in the wind, but we had the roof on by then and a tin stove with plenty of firewood, and we were snug at night. Dill arrived before the snow was too deep for wagons, just after we had driven the last nail. His timing could not have been better.

My work was finished and I now had a decision to make,

though it really wasn't much of decision at all, considering the options. I could either spend the winter at the lake or go somewhere else. But where would I go this late in the year? I could buy a horse and ride to Edmonton, but what was there? An economically depressed town, a curmudgeonly Scotsman at the fort and precious little else. Fort Pitt was attractive with Amelia being there, but there was no guarantee of work and I couldn't expect them to feed me for the winter. Battleford was reachable but held little appeal. Both Cameron and Dill had said I could stay with them, despite the cramped conditions it would create. Then, out of the blue, a solution presented itself.

James Simpson, the agent from the Hudson's Bay Company store down the road, was required in Fort Pitt for a lengthy period and asked Cameron, for whom he had great respect, to replace him in his absence. Cameron didn't have to think about it. It was a chance for a steady income over the winter rather than the capricious business of a free trader. And since staying in partnership with Dill would have been a conflict of interest, the two men worked out an amicable parting and this left the door wide open for me. It was wonderful how things kept falling into place.

Dill and I quickly reached an agreement by which I would work for him as a clerk in the store for a small salary and commission on any items that I sold. It benefited him more than me but I didn't care. I was young, inexperienced, willing to learn and happy with what I got. I was also happy about being at the lake, living in the small settlement of log houses and with people who had almost become a surrogate family to me.

John and Theresa Delaney lived across the road and

invited me over for a meal from time to time. John was the farming instructor for the Indians; Theresa was like a mother to me and I could always depend on being the lucky recipient of her baking. Next to the Delaneys was the North-West Mounted Police barracks housing six policemen under the command of Corporal Ralph Sleigh, the man who had unsuccessfully tried to arrest Man Who Speaks Another Tongue on Poundmaker's reserve. He was a stern individual but scrupulously fair. Adjacent to the barracks was John Pritchard's house. He was country-born, meaning his father was from the British Isles and his mother Indian, and employed by the government as an interpreter, but he kept a rooming house on the side. He had a wife and two small boys. Up the road from Dill and me was a Catholic church with a detached manse housing the priest, Father Leon Fafard. With him lived a much older man, a mechanic named John Williscraft. The only crick in the neck of this fine body of people was Tom Quinn. He lived just down from the Delaneys with his plump Cree wife, their eight-year-old daughter and an assistant named Charlie Gouin.

Then there were the several hundred reasons why each one of us was there in the first place: Lucky Man's band of Woods Cree who lived in log houses on the shores of the lake, north of us, and Big Bear's band in their lodges on the bank of Frog Creek, to the south. Everyone, with the possible exception of the Bear, was poised to take advantage of this burgeoning area; we all expected to see the telegraph arrive in one year and the railroad in three.

November fled into December as I slowly learned the

trading business. Dill taught me about the variety of animal skins that came into the store and how to grade them. These were mainly beaver skins but muskrat, fox and most of the other animals indigenous to the area came in as well. Much of their value was based on their "primeness," or how thick and luxurious the pelt was. Animal furs came into prime at varying times over the winter: fox were earlier than beaver, which were earlier than muskrat and so on. Colour and texture were also important, and size was a consideration. Top-quality pelts were "Ones"; those that were rubbed or slightly damaged were "Seconds"; and anything in worse condition was considered "Low-grade." If there was anything I wasn't sure about, I could ask Dill, but I got fairly adept at it with practice. Cameron was also helpful, considering we were his competitors.

Christmas approached. The feasting and merriment would be much better at Fort Pitt, Cameron declared, and he was going to take McLean up on his invitation to spend a few days there. I was welcome to join him if I wanted, so when Dill said he was more than happy to stay and keep the store open, it was all the incentive I needed. I looked forward to seeing Amelia again.

Cameron and I borrowed one of the NWMP's one-horse open sleighs, wrapped our lower bodies in warm blankets and left before dawn on December 23. We followed the many small frozen lakes between our community and the fort, stopping briefly at Onion Lake for warm drinks, and to rest and feed the horse. Our host at the settlement, the Anglican minister Charles Quinney, was also preparing to attend the celebrations at Pitt. Beyond Onion Lake, the sun blazed in a brilliant blue sky and the air was brittle with cold but utterly still, with snow crusting everything. It was a spectacular setting for our journey. Darkness had descended around us by the time we arrived at our destination.

People poured in from smaller, outlying posts until there was quite a crowd lodged in the guest quarters and in every other space where a body could bed down for the night. Cameron and I bunked in the police barracks.

On Christmas morning, while those with families and children opened gifts, Stanley Simpson, the fort's accountant, invited Cameron and me to join him while he checked his trap line. Simpson was meticulous in everything he did, from keeping the Company's books to his deportment and the way he dressed. In a country where the norm was mud-spattered or dusty clothes, and plenty of dirt under the fingernails, Simpson managed to look as if he had just come from the haberdashers and stopped in for a haircut on the way. Like Cameron, he was smooth-shaven when most of the white men in the Territories had moustaches or beards.

Many of the fort's employees had trap lines, an endeavour heartily endorsed by the Company. Not only did it give them something to do in their spare time, it also supplemented their modest incomes. Of course, it added to the purse of the Company, for it bought the furs and then sold them at a profit. For me it was a unique opportunity to learn something new, so I accepted the invitation with enthusiasm.

We donned snowshoes and crossed the frozen North Saskatchewan, climbed the benches on the south side and headed east. Simpson might have been an accountant but he was as fit as an athlete; it took all the strength and speed Cameron and I possessed just to keep up with him. We did a seven-mile loop and the traps yielded two red foxes and a cross fox, all of which would fetch a tidy sum. Simpson was delighted with "Nature's Christmas presents," as he put it.

We arrived back at the fort in time for lunch and after that the men joined McLean in his office where we drank tots of brandy and those so inclined smoked cheroots. Later, all the adults went outside for the "Battle of the Bunnies." An annual feature on Christmas Day at the fort, the battle involved two opposing teams, each member armed with a rifle. The object was to kill as many rabbits as possible in a specified time and the team with the most kills was the winner. While it was great fun, it served a practical purpose by keeping down the rabbit population, which in some years was overwhelming.

Amelia was on the opposing team and shouldered and shot her rifle almost as well as the men. As in cribbage and checkers, she was very competitive. I spoke to her only briefly and she said she was glad that I had come.

After the battle, there were snowball fights and races until dark. Then several dozen people retired to the gaily decorated reception hall for a grand dinner of wild rice soup, roast prairie chicken and partridge, and roast beaver that reminded me of lamb, all superbly done by Bob Hodson, the McLeans' diminutive, squinty-eyed English cook, and his assistants, namely Amelia, her sisters and their mother, Helen. Dessert, besides cakes and pies, was plum pudding smothered in brandy sauce. For many, it was a taste of home and the day wouldn't have been Christmas without it. With dinner over, the men gathered again in McLean's office for more brandy and cheroots, then returned to the reception hall and played "Pass the Button" and "Post Office" with the ladies and children. Once the small children had retired for the night, the evening grew mellow. The McLean girls gathered around the organ and while Amelia played that, Eliza bowed the fiddle and Kitty strummed the banjo, and they led us in singing the most popular carols. I nudged Cameron and told him that he should get his violin and join in but he said that he preferred solos in quieter places and with fewer people around.

Outside, it had begun to snow, huge flakes that gathered on the cross-pieces of the mullioned windows. I had never experienced such a happy Christmas, yet when I went to bed, I felt melancholy and lonely, worrying about my mother and how she was faring with my father. And, for the first time, missing home. I wondered how Ma had kept Christmas, and if she had received my letter. Six months had passed since I last saw her and any number of things could have happened. I wrote her another letter, a note, really, and hoped it would reach her.

Meanwhile, there were so many people around that Amelia and I easily managed a walk on our own along the riverbank. It was bold of her because she hadn't asked for permission, but she wasn't worried. Her father considered me a responsible, hard-working young man and she doubted that he would object too strenuously should he find out. And it was, after all, Christmas.

We knew vaguely of each other's pasts from our evenings in the reception hall, so with the New Year nearly upon us we talked mainly of our plans for the future. I told her of the ranch that I wanted to own one day and of the country I had seen coming out of the mountains, and how seamlessly the two would fit together. She spoke of her love of music and writing poetry, and of her real passion: languages. She was already translating some old ballads into Cree, and wanted eventually to include the Longfellow poem, *The Bridge*, despite its length and difficulty. She hoped to find work as a translator, perhaps for the recently created government department responsible for Indian affairs.

Our conversation continued in that vein over the brief duration of our walk. I liked Amelia, as I'm sure she liked me, but I think we intuitively realized that if our genders and youth had brought us together, other factors would keep us apart. I'm not sure either of us thought about such things then, nor could we have articulated them if we had, but there was no awkwardness or discomfort in the truth of it. We simply enjoyed each other's company.

On New Year's Eve, many more people arrived for the celebration, including most of the folks from Frog Lake. Even Tom Quinn came with his wife. The NWMP provided the festivities, food and drink just as the Company had provided the Christmas fare. We danced to music played by an impromptu band until we were ready to drop—cotillions, reels, waltzes and polkas, even the Red River jig, played by a Métis man while the white fiddlers watched in amazement. One of those was Cameron who told me that he did not know of a white musician who was able to master that style of playing. Not only was the fingering intricate, the energy of the man was volcanic—he danced on the spot while he played. I had never seen a more exciting fiddler.

Amelia was much in demand as a partner but I managed more than my share of dances with her. Those moments when an arm was slipped around a waist or over a shoulder, when hands clasped tightly, were delightful.

When midnight arrived, the music stopped abruptly and the men once more retired to McLean's office for cheroots, this time complemented by well-aged Scotch instead of brandy. We toasted the New Year and wished each other prosperity, and the others filled the room with smoke and reminiscences of the past year. I had no stories to tell that would interest these men so I kept silent and enjoyed just being there. Indeed, I could think of no place I'd rather have been than in that room with those men sharing the camaraderie of the moment. Then McLean broke the spell.

"Well, gentlemen," he said. "I suppose we ought to get back to the ladies."

We danced through the night until the band gave up in exhaustion. By then, we had barely enough energy to form a circle and render a discordant version of "Auld Lang Syne," following the Scottish tradition of singing it at the end of the party rather than at midnight. Then we dragged ourselves off to our respective beds. I'd had a bit more to drink than I should have and slept the dreamless sleep of the alcoholically saturated. When I awoke beneath a warm blanket and not chained to a stump, I felt as if I'd got away with something.

Cameron and I spent New Year's Day recovering from the festivities and left for Frog Lake the following morning. Amelia herself packed us more than enough food for the trip and she and her family said goodbye with hopes that they would see us at Easter.

JANUARY WAS long and bitterly cold, February less so. Trade was slow at the store, so in my spare time I helped Charlie Gouin to construct the agency buildings. John Delaney was sometimes there and that usually meant an invitation to have lunch or supper with him and Theresa, something only a fool would turn down. Theresa was fair haired and short but robust, a woman who loved to see her men fed and enjoyed cooking for them. If she suspected you had one square inch of empty space left in your belly she would heap more food on your plate, presuming your protestations meant exactly the opposite. "Eat up," she'd say. "A man can't do the work God intended him to do on an empty stomach."

It was just as hard to do it on a bulging stomach, but that was Theresa.

She and John, who were both in their early 40s, had come from the east in 1882, first by train to the railhead, near the Manitoba border, and then by buckboard, camping all the way. She loved her life here and thought the Indians were the luckiest people in the world. She said to me, "If any Scotch, English or Irish farmer had the advantage given the Indians, he'd consider himself fortunate indeed."

"What do you mean?" I asked.

"I mean the handouts the government gives them. They

are given food and paid to clear their own land. If their crops fail they are given more food. Who could reasonably ask for more?"

"But isn't that just to help them out until they can do it on their own?" I remembered what Cameron had told me and added, "And you can't expect them to learn in a couple of years what we've had hundreds of years to learn."

"You've been talking to Bill Cameron," she said, as if that made my counter argument irrelevant. I said no more because her big heart overrode her narrow view of the world.

John, a brooding, quiet man, was of a similar mind to his wife and while he and I got along famously, I learned that the Indians held him in low regard. He had once refused rations to two of them and they had horsewhipped him. The pair was sent to jail in Edmonton for their crime and John dug in his heels even further, making few concessions. The Indians also said he had taken liberties with more than one of their young women during his first year in the settlement. I don't know how much truth there was to the accusation, only that it was not a subject one could easily broach in the white community. In those days wives often turned a blind eye to their husband's improprieties because it would have been a strong woman indeed to presume she could face this land on her own.

Sometimes I would skate a couple of miles down Frog Creek to visit the latest arrivals in the area: John Gowanlock, his wife, Mary, and Gowanlock's clerk, Bill Gilchrist. The Gowanlocks were newlyweds from Ontario who had arrived in January and were building a sawmill, after which they were going to erect a gristmill in order to provide both lumber and flour to the Indians. Once those operations were under way, Gilchrist was planning to enter Manitoba College as a theology student and return to minister to the Indians. All three were fine people and about the same age as Cameron, who quickly befriended them.

John played the concertina and Mary sang in a sweet, clear voice that made me think of angels. She was slender and very pretty, with long black hair, lovely brown eyes and an oval face that seemed as fragile as porcelain. I thought Cameron, who often accompanied me on my visits, liked her more than he ever let on. Many were the times I glanced his way only to find him staring at Mary. I can't say that I blamed him; she made a very pleasing sight for any man's eyes. I enjoyed my visits with the Gowanlocks immensely. Theirs was a neat and orderly world, the house trim and warm, a most agreeable contrast to the bachelor conditions in which I lived.

Cameron was the first to take me into Big Bear's camp, which straddled the creek halfway between the settlement and the Gowanlocks' house. Later, I would go on my own and it always astonished me how few men there were in the camp. Granted, many were out working, but women and children, and dogs that looked more like timber wolves, prevailed. In fact, when I mentioned this to Tom Quinn he said that when he paid annuities to Big Bear's band, as well as Lucky Man's, there were 135 women, 162 boys and 149 girls. The men numbered only 58. Nevertheless, there was always something thrilling about entering the encampment: the general din of the children; the yelping, slinking dogs lurking everywhere, hoping for some fish or rabbit offal to be discarded; the conical lodges made of buffalo hides, the poles poking out of the blackened smoke-holes at angles to each other, always 15 of them and each one with its own name—"Love," "Respect," "Faith," "Happiness" and so on. The relationship between all these things was where the poles intersected. Fourteen horizontal pins, like ladder rungs, above and below the door, bound the hides and kept the lodge intact, just as a family must remain intact. The doors themselves faced the rising sun. Such things I learned, and more, with each visit.

I was always made welcome in Big Bear's lodge and without fail he would ask, *"Asay cî kiya kîkîmîcison?"*—"Have you eaten yet?" There wasn't much big game around, so it was usually a rabbit cooking in a blackened kettle over a fire in the centre of the lodge. He made the offer even when there was scarcely enough food for his own people, and to refuse it would have been an insult. His generosity in the face of such privation humbled me. He always sat facing the lodge door, leaning against a backrest made of willow, and would bid me sit down and smoke the *calumet* or pipe with him. His wives and children sat and lay helter-skelter around the fire. Not once did I ever see either him or his wives discipline the smaller children, which is not to say they didn't hear endless stories of the difference between acceptable and unacceptable behavior. His two oldest sons, King Bird and Little Bad Man, were sometimes there, though they had families of their own, and another, Horse Child, was always around. He was about 10 or 11 years old and took a shine to me; I learned many Cree words and a few games from him.

A rift existed between Big Bear and Little Bad Man, who

had been difficult to get along with even as a child, hence his name. He was contrary and militant, and disagreed with his father's stance of peace and negotiations. In the recent past, his dissatisfaction had caused him to take 50 of his father's followers down to Montana to live and he would never have come back had he not been expelled from the United States by American soldiers. Because of his disloyalty, Big Bear had passed him over when he was appointing councillors. Little Bad Man still harboured a grudge over that; nevertheless, he was usually friendly toward me, as was King Bird.

The only times I ever felt uncomfortable were when Wandering Spirit, Miserable Man or Man Who Speaks Another Tongue were in camp. All three would have waged war against the whites with little provocation. This was especially true of Man Who Speaks Another Tongue, ever since the incident involving the Indian agent and that warrior's subsequent imprisonment by Crozier. I believe all three men viewed me as an intruder and therefore did nothing to make me feel welcome.

As time passed I picked up a working knowledge of the Cree language and by March, though far from fluent, I could at least grasp the gist of a conversation and sometimes make myself understood. Best of all, I got to know Big Bear, or Mistahi-maskwa, his Cree name. I called him Ne-moo-soom, or Grandfather, which was a sign of respect.

He was a man of about 60 years, although his face made him appear much older. It was as creased as the bark of an old oak tree, scarred by smallpox, and the sun and wind had burned it nearly black. Dark, puffy eyes restlessly roamed the horizon when he was outside, and a slightly turned-down mouth gave a hint of sadness to a resolute jaw. He kept his hair in two braids that came down in front of his shoulders and wore a leather shirt and leggings with a blue breechclout. In cold weather he wrapped a striped Hudson's Bay Company blanket around his thick chest with the end thrown over his left shoulder. Most whites would have considered him ugly, as I did at first, but the inner man shone through with such a proud, intelligent radiance that those who got to know him were blinded to his physical qualities. And I remember most of all his magnificent voice, a magnet that drew the ear, and his eloquence. I could sit and listen to him talk for hours, which he was quite capable of doing, even though I understood little of what he said at first. Some men are born to the task of leadership and Big Bear was one of them. In the larger world he might have been a prime minister or president.

The Bear, as most whites called him, was a man comfortable in his own skin. He had wanted nothing more than to carry on with the old ways of trailing the buffalo, and it was a great source of frustration for him that it was no longer an option. Those who followed him shared that feeling. Many had come from bands on reserve, unwilling to accept a sedentary life. He also drew the disaffected, men like Wandering Spirit and Man Who Speaks Another Tongue, who were spoiling for a fight. Whereas most bands had only a dozen or so lodges, Big Bear's had more than a hundred. But he and his people were hungry, living mainly on rabbits and whatever else they could scrounge to keep from starving. Not only was it a life to which they were totally unaccustomed, it placed them in the undesirable position of needing the white man and, to make matters worse, the Bear had to deal with Tom Quinn's stinginess.

The agent met every request for food with his own rule: "No work, no food," so some band members worked on the gristmill or the agency buildings while others ran freight between Edmonton and Fort Pitt. Some cut wood around the camp, which they found objectionable, not because of the physical labour involved but because there was a rumour around the community that once Big Bear moved to his reserve some 35 miles to the west, Quinn and John Delaney were going to buy the cleared land and sell it to settlers at a sizeable profit. In other words, they were getting cheap labour and Quinn was using the rations to which they were entitled as a means of manipulating them. Big Bear went to Fort Pitt a couple of times over the winter to complain but McLean could do little to help him, only pass on his concerns to Government House in Fort Battleford where the typical response was silence.

Big Bear had held out against signing Treaty Six as long as he could. He believed it was a trap and that the incentive gifts offered by the government were bait. He told the men sent to negotiate with him, "When an Indian sets a trap he scatters bait around it and when the fox comes to take it he is banged on the head. We want no bait."

He worked hard to unify the Indians, not to rise up against the white man but to regain control over their own lives. He saw those on reserves as complacent wards of the government and had gone to Poundmaker's reserve, not only for the Thirst Dance, but to convince him of that truth. There was also to be a huge council meeting involving more than 2,000 Indians from which he hoped unification would ultimately arise. After the Thirst Dance, he had met with Louis Riel in Prince Albert and was impressed, seeing first-hand how incensed the rebel leader was over the treatment of the Métis at the hands of white men. Riel spoke of unity, too, but so far Big Bear was still treading water, a patient man while others around him were not. Wandering Spirit and Miserable Man in particular, and even Little Bad Man, had run out of patience some time ago.

It pleased me immensely when the Bear was in camp and not away hunting or trapping, even more when he stopped by Cameron's for supper. I always made a point of inviting myself if Cameron forgot. Big Bear would regale us for an hour or two with tales of buffalo hunts, riding among the stampeding herds with bows and arrows, each hunter dropping two or three beasts before they escaped. Best of all were his tales of war with the Blackfoot. He would begin all his stories with "*Kayas*," or "Long ago," and I remember one in particular.

He and Sweet Grass, accompanied by 18 warriors, had entered Blackfoot territory to capture horses when they came across one of their enemy herding his animals down into a river valley. They chased him and stumbled upon a Blackfoot camp. All of a sudden, the tables were turned and they were running for their lives. They reached a spruce grove and dug in for a fight. The Blackfoot quickly surrounded them and they exchanged gunfire throughout the remainder of that day and on into the next. Late the following morning, the Blackfoot had lost so many men, including a chief, that they withdrew. Big Bear and Sweet Grass had not lost any men although one had received a shoulder wound and another had a shattered spine. When they left, they could not take the seriously injured warrior with them. He asked if they were leaving him there to die and they said no, they were only going to find some food and water. But they never went back for him.

"You left him there?" I asked, appalled by the apparent callousness of it.

"We had no choice," Big Bear said. "Even if we could have carried him he would have died from his wound. By telling him that we were coming back, he at least died with hope in his heart."

The Bear paused, his face stoical. "Those days are gone now and it is good. No longer does Cree and Blackfoot blood soak the prairie. We have smoked the pipe of peace and for that my heart rests easy."

In March, the snow began disappearing from the low ridges in the vicinity of Frog Lake and while the weather turned mild, relations between the South Saskatchewan River Métis and government forces grew more volatile, like dry prairie grass that required only a small spark to set it blazing. In the settlement, everyone knew that runners had come to Frog Lake on behalf of Riel, seeking Big Bear's help once more. None of us knew what his reply had been; we only knew that he was not a man who saw violence as a means to an end. We trusted him in that regard.

On a grey wintry day near the end of March, Cameron came barging into our store, his face a map of concern. He had just come from Big Bear's camp and was more excited than I'd ever seen him. The Bear was away hunting, hoping to get a moose because Quinn still refused him an ox, but his warriors, led by Wandering Spirit, were in council and Cameron had found them extremely guarded in everything they said. The tension in the lodge was as taut as a fiddle string and Cameron quickly realized that he wasn't welcome.

"Something's up," he told us. "I don't know what it is but something important has happened and I'm sure Wandering Spirit is in charge of the camp. I'd stake a year's salary on it."

If Wandering Spirit was in charge, it meant that Big Bear, who was the political chief, had conceded power to his war chief and that the Cree had serious intentions of going to war.

Business at Dill's store and the Company's store virtually stopped, which confirmed Cameron's suspicions. Yet no news was forthcoming from Fort Pitt. Had the rebellion started? Was the fort itself under attack? Why had the Indians here not tried anything? They could easily have overwhelmed us had they wanted to. Quinn tried to extract information from them but they would tell him nothing. Big Bear was still away. So we stewed for three days, not knowing what was up. Then around suppertime, Billy Anderson, a police constable, rode in on a steaming horse, having covered the 35 miles from Fort Pitt in three hours. He brought with him the news we half expected but did not want to hear.

Superintendent Crozier and a contingent of policemen, aided by a small volunteer force from Prince Albert, had confronted Louis Riel and his rebels, some of them Cree, at a place called Duck Lake, a few miles east of Fort Carlton. After the ensuing battle, 14 men lay dead. The rebellion had indeed begun in earnest and Frog Lake was no longer considered a safe place to be. A message from Inspector Dickens suggested that all of the white residents evacuate the community immediately and make haste to Fort Pitt. If we did not want to, then he would send his detachment to protect our settlement. We would have to make up our minds quickly, whichever course we chose. A delay might result in regrettable consequences.

EIGHT

Lunar Eclipse

THE AIR IN THE ROOM WAS hot and close, thick with pipe smoke and body odour. All of the whites in Frog Lake had gathered in John and Theresa Delaney's house to discuss Dickens's message, viewed by some as an emergency. It was near midnight and Theresa served tea and coffee strong enough to make sleep a far-off country.

Tom Quinn was speaking. "I suppose if we had any sense we would pull out of here before daylight. All of us."

Cameron said, "You can go if you like, but I'm staying."

I wondered if he was joking but his face said that he wasn't.

"There are a lot of furs and supplies at the store," he continued, "and I'm responsible for them. I've not received orders from Mr. Simpson that I can leave. Billy Anderson brought mail from the fort and there was nothing in it telling me to go. So I'm staying."

"It could be your life that's at stake here. Is it worth less than the Company's inventory?"

This was Quinn, his voice rising above others. Despite his arrogance, I could understand why the agent would support evacuating Frog Lake. He had told me one night over tea about the Minnesota Massacre, when the Sioux rose up and slaughtered several hundred whites, including his father. Quinn was lucky and barely escaped with his life.

Cameron knew this story as well as anybody, but he had made up his mind. "I consider the Indians my friends and I don't think I have anything to fear. But if you don't feel safe here, or any of the rest of you, for that matter," he said, gesturing to everyone in the room, "then you ought to leave."

Father Fafard spoke. "I have to agree with Cameron. If you feel threatened, then you should go. But I think it would be a mistake to abandon the community, because then we abandon the Indians as well. And for what? A skirmish that happened 200 miles from here and has nothing to do with us. We've all worked hard to prove our faith in these people, so why throw it all out the window? That frightens me more than the possibility of being killed."

Father Felix Marchand, a wiry, energetic man who was Fafard's assistant and provided services at Onion Lake, concurred. "It's the half-breeds who are in revolt, not the Indians. We must show them our trust."

"Then maybe we should take Dickens up on his offer," interjected Delaney, his long, narrow face flushed red from the heat and the dilemma. "We might be able to rely on Big Bear to maintain some common sense but I'm not sure we can say the same about Wandering Spirit and Miserable Man."

"How can Dickens help us?" asked Cameron. "He only has about 25 men and he'd have to leave more than half of them behind to guard the fort." He nodded toward Ralph Sleigh. "Add that to Ralph's two men and you've got a dozen or so policemen up against hundreds of Indians. It makes more sense to me to send the Frog Lake detachment to Fort Pitt because . . ."

Murmurs of dissent rose from the group, interrupting Cameron.

"Hear me out," he said, his voice rising above the others. "The way I see it is that the Cree don't like the police, because the police are always giving them trouble. If there aren't any police around, there's no excuse to pick a fight. I think we'd all be safer without them."

I noticed, as I'm sure others did, that he didn't mention the Indians' dislike of Quinn—they always called him "Dog Agent" or "The Bully" behind his back—and that perhaps he should go too. But his presence wasn't as conspicuous as the Mounties' and besides, he was in the room and Cameron was undoubtedly being diplomatic.

Quinn said, "I think that Father Fafard has a valid point. So has Cameron." He turned to Sleigh. "There's no point in making the Indians any angrier than they already are. Maybe the first step to take is for you to leave."

Sleigh looked around at the others. "Is that how everyone feels?"

There were bobbing heads and a few murmured, "Yes."

They apparently saw the wisdom in Cameron's suggestion and agreed with the priest that they had invested too much time and money in the community to abandon it unless it became absolutely necessary.

"Whatever you wish, then," Sleigh said with a curt nod of his head. "We'll leave first thing in the morning."

"I'd make it before dawn, if I were you," said Quinn. "If the Indians get wind that you're leaving they might try to stop you."

Cameron told Sleigh that he had two kegs of powder and 80 pounds of ball at the store that he was concerned might fall into Indian hands if the present situation deteriorated. Would Sleigh have extra room in his sleigh to take it with him?

"We'll *make* room for it," he said.

Constable Larry Loasby and I went with Cameron to the Company store for the ammunition. My knees were quaking, my mind awhirl at the possibility of a fight. *Well*, I thought, *isn't that what you came for?* Yet now I wasn't so sure. It's much easier to wage war against people you don't know and I had come to know Big Bear and his family well, and gained a great deal of respect for them. I suppose I could have taken the easy way out by leaving with the police but the thought of being branded a coward by either the whites or the Indians held me back. All I could do was ride the thing out, placing my trust in Cameron's judgment and in Big Bear. Once he returned from hunting, the chief's cool head would prevail. That's what I hoped, anyway.

Cameron did not think that we should get rid of all the powder and bullets. "I need to have some here in case the

Indians come around. If I don't, they'll suspect we don't trust them. This will let them know that we do."

It made sense to me and apparently Loasby as well, because he didn't argue the point.

We hauled the rest to the police barracks and Cameron, knowing that the Company would eventually demand a full accounting of the post's inventory, had Sleigh sign for it. Both Cameron and I were too keyed up to sleep so, while most of the others had gone home to bed, we stayed to help the police load their double sleigh and a couple of pack horses. We emptied their office of all records and the barracks of all personal belongings, bedding and food, anything that the Indians might be able to use in the event of a rebellion. An hour before dawn, in a heavy snowfall, Corporal Sleigh whipped the horses into motion and the overloaded sleigh, along with two mounted policemen leading the packhorses, slipped as quietly as they could out of Frog Lake. I had a hollow feeling in my stomach as I watched them go.

On the way back to the store, I told Cameron that I was a little worried.

"If you're worried, you'll be on your guard and that's not a bad thing, Jack. It won't hurt any of us to keep our eyes open."

He'd no sooner got the words out of his mouth than I caught some movement out of the corner of my eye. "Jesus!" I said. "Look over there!"

A shadowy figure was hurrying along the road toward Big Bear's camp. We were certain it was one of his men wrapped in a blanket.

"They've been watching us all along," Cameron said. "We should have known better! Well, they were bound to find out that the police were gone sooner or later. I wonder how Wandering Spirit will take the news?"

"I guess he'll let us know when he's ready," I said, with more bravado than I felt.

Cameron and I parted company and I went to my room where Dill was fast asleep. I climbed into bed but had a hard time settling down. Once I did, I don't think I slept much longer than a half-hour and I dreamed of Indians. Not the ones I had come to know, but of savage, bloodthirsty, dime-novel Indians. And Wild Jack Strong was nowhere about. It startled me awake and I was disoriented in the grey light of the room until I heard Dill's quiet snoring. Despite its soothing effect sleep was impossible, and rather than lie there and toss and turn, I arose, dressed and went to see if Cameron was up. He had more savvy about Indians than most of the others in the community, with the possible exception of Tom Quinn, and I felt safer in his presence. Besides, the Indians liked him, and that was more important than anything else.

When I arrived at his quarters, Cameron was already up and about. He hadn't slept much either and was just about ready to go down and open the store.

"I don't know why," he said, "but I suppose we ought to show the Indians, if any of them come around, that it's business as usual. Is Dill opening up?"

"He's still sleeping," I said.

"Wonderful! The Company hates competition."

While Cameron opened the store I went around to the side and brought in an armful of wood for the stove. Dill was up and had come outside. He saw me and waved. Over by the road were several Indians, among them Wandering Spirit and Little Bad Man. Then I saw Quinn coming from the other direction with one of Big Bear's men, who left him and came over to the store. He told us that Quinn was going to meet with the war chief and other Indian leaders at John Delaney's house, and the agent suggested that it might be a good idea if Cameron joined them.

"You might as well tag along, Jack," Cameron said to me. "You need to know what's going on as much as the rest of us."

A couple of inches of snow had fallen since the police left but I doubted it would last because the morning was warming up.

Everyone seemed to be in a good mood when we arrived, including Wandering Spirit and the three other council members in attendance—Little Bad Man, Four Sky Thunder and Miserable Man. The war chief grinned broadly and said, "Big-Lie Day!" I thought at first he was accusing us of being liars but when everybody laughed, I realized that he was referring to the fact that it was April 1, or April Fool's Day. Nobody seemed in the right frame of mind for practical jokes, though.

They really didn't need us there at all, but Little Bad Man, whose eyes always made him look as if he were on the verge of a smile, rose and offered his chair to either Cameron or me. Cameron placed his hand on the Indian's shoulder and said in Cree, "Thank you, my brother. But I would be remiss if I took the chair of a guest." He motioned the Indian back in the chair, saying, "Please."

Satisfied with the exchange, Little Bad Man sat down and addressed Quinn. "Sioux Speaker, the half-breeds have given us bad advice this winter. They said they would spill much blood and wanted us to join them. As you know, they have beaten the police at Duck Lake and killed many. We do not want to join them. We want to stay here and be your friends. We ask that if the police come to fight us, you will speak on our behalf and protect us."

Little Bad Man's statement pleased Quinn. He was still in control here as far as he was concerned and he preferred it that way.

"I like your talk, Imasees [Little Bad Man]," he said. "It is good talk, good that you want to remain our friends. If you stay in your camp, I'll see that no one bothers you. You will not want for food, either. Naturally, I can only talk to Big Bear about that. So he must come and see me as soon as he returns."

The pledge of food brought smiles to the Indians' faces, all except Miserable Man, who rarely smiled about anything. He and the other councillors left after shaking hands with everyone and on the way out he said something to Quinn that I didn't catch.

There was a buoyant feeling in the room. It seemed our fears were unfounded and that the Indians did not intend to join the rebellion. Quinn's offer of food had most likely sealed the deal. Cameron asked the agent what Miserable Man had said to him.

"Nothing, really. A remark in jest about the threat he made to me in Fort Pitt. I think it's his way of apologizing. Anyway, they all seem friendly enough. I still think we need to keep an eye on Wandering Spirit, though, at least until Big Bear gets back. If he stays calm we should be all right."

In the afternoon, Big Bear returned from his hunting trip and I think all the whites in the settlement were a little less tense. We were now even more convinced that nothing bad would happen, that we were safe.

Later that evening we were sitting with Quinn in his office when Big Bear and Little Bad Man dropped in. They sat down and the Bear looked tired and uncomfortable in the straight-back chair. He spoke of how frustrating the hunt had been for him. He had wanted to bring back a moose to feed his people but had seen nothing and returned empty-handed. His people, he knew, had expected better results from their chief and were disappointed. It had put him in a melancholy mood. Still, Little Bad Man had told him of Quinn's earlier promise of food and now he would like the agent to fulfill it.

"The food will be yours in time, Mistahi-maskwa," Quinn said. "But I can't give it to you without a valid reason. The government would be angry. You must first show that you deserve it."

Little Bad Man responded. "I have not forgotten what you said this morning. Now you say that you need a good reason to give us food. Is our hunger not a good reason?"

Before Quinn could say anything, Big Bear said angrily, "I told you at Fort Pitt that I would have you replaced but I did nothing about it. Now I think it is time that you left. But you must leave the storehouse open so that we can have what is rightfully ours."

Quinn scoffed at such a preposterous notion. "I'll do no such thing!"

Sensing that arguing would get him nowhere, Big Bear switched tactics. He said that he had heard rumours that something had happened at Duck Lake. Did the agent have any details?

"Rumours?" Quinn was surprised at the question. "You know full well what happened there!"

Of course, Big Bear knew. How could he not? I think what he wanted was to hear it from Quinn's mouth, wanted to hear the agent admit that a handful of Métis and Indians had easily defeated the police, and that he would put two and two together. But if Quinn got it, he didn't let on and read the part of the message from Inspector Dickens that said he would bring his detachment here to protect the settlement.

"Five summers ago I met Riel below the Medicine Line," Big Bear said when the agent had finished. "He told me that much blood would flow and that it could not be helped. I hope it will not be true, for even if it is Riel's way, it is not mine. Yet I had a dream, an ugly dream. I saw a spring shooting up out of the ground. I covered it with my hand, trying to smother it, but it spurted up between my fingers and ran over the back of my hand. It was a spring of blood, Sioux Speaker!"

With that, the old chief rose abruptly and said, "Good night." He shook Quinn's hand, then Cameron's and mine.

I gazed into his eyes and saw a weariness that I had not seen before, as if events were now beyond his control, and there was a distinct pressure in his grip that might have been friendship or a final farewell. He and his son left.

"That sounded like a thinly disguised warning to me," Cameron said to Quinn.

The agent, however, did not appear overly worried. He reckoned that Wandering Spirit and Miserable Man were still his primary concerns, and had they not been more than friendly this morning?

Cameron wasn't so sure. "Something's troubling Big Bear and it's not just a lack of food. There's more to what he said than just the words he used," he said. "I think he was telling us that he's not in control anymore. If he isn't, then Wandering Spirit and the other war chiefs are. I'm still not entirely sure that most of us here have much to worry about but it could be a different story for you, Tom. You know as well as I do what the Indians think of you. You're the man who always says 'no' and that means that you could be in danger."

It needed to be said and Cameron had said it tactfully. Quinn merely shrugged and smiled. "They can kill me," he said, "but they can't scare me."

This sort of verbal swaggering was typical of Quinn. Cameron pressed his point, suggesting that perhaps it truly was time for him to leave. "It could be the best thing for everyone," he insisted. "For exactly the same reasons the police left."

Quinn's presence bothered me, too, and I had kept quiet

long enough. I said, "Bill's right, Tom. You're putting everyone in danger. I'm all for you going, too."

Quinn's eyes flickered in my direction. He addressed us both. "That's what they want me to do but I'm not giving in to them. Not now. Not ever. I'll be damned if I'll go!" he said. That was the end of the conversation as far as the agent was concerned. He stood up. "I think we'd all better get some rest." He saw Cameron and me to the door and bade us good night.

Quinn was an enigma. There wasn't a sympathetic bone in his body for the Indians, even though he had Indian blood and was married to a Cree woman. I mentioned this to Cameron as we walked home.

"Women are few and far between in this country," he said. "And I guess some men need female company more than others. As for the way he looks down his nose at the Indians, I don't know. Maybe he thinks if he's mean enough to them, we'll all forget that he's part Indian himself."

The trail back to our quarters was soggy with melting snow as the temperature was quite mild, the air moist. After an overcast day with intermittent rain, the sky was now a patchwork of stars and clouds. For a while the moon was revealed, with the shadow of the Earth half across it. The inclement weather, combined with concern for our plight, had made us forget the predicted partial lunar eclipse but it seemed ominous. We stopped and watched until a cloud obscured our view.

It appeared that everyone in the community had gone to bed, except the Delaneys at whose house a light shone from a kitchen window. The Gowanlocks were staying with them and my guess was that they were still up talking, perhaps hoping to catch a glimpse of the eclipse. When I'd seen them in the afternoon they were all in high spirits and certain there was nothing to worry about.

Cameron and I walked in silence, lost in thought. At first the sound didn't register in our tired brains, then there it was, off in the distance, coming from the direction of Big Bear's camp. The muted sound of drums.

"I think a nightcap might be in order, Jack," Cameron said. "Interested?"

Cameron was not a drinking man, so I presumed that he found the drums as unsettling as I did. "Sure," I said. "Something about the size of Frog Lake ought to do just fine."

We both laughed but there was no humour in it.

I was exhausted and ready for bed, and so was Cameron, but the drums woke us both up. We ascended the small rise on which the Company store sat and climbed the stairs to his room above. I waited at the door while he struck a match to find the lamp and light it. Our shadows all but filled the small, slope-ceilinged room. Cameron poured two large brandies and handed one to me. It wasn't the size of the lake but it was a damned fine start. He sat on his cot, his back against the wall, while I made myself comfortable in a wooden rocker. The room was chilly despite the spring-like air outside but neither of us felt like lighting a fire. I pulled the blanket resting on the back of the rocker down over my shoulders and Cameron laid one from the bed over his chest. We let the brandy do the rest and raised our glasses to each other in a silent toast. The liquor slid easily down my throat and a lovely warmth spread through my body.

"I just don't know, Jack," Cameron said. "I'm trying to decide whether or not Quinn's first instincts were right and that I really am a bloody fool. What do you think?"

"I don't like the sound of those drums one bit, but at least they haven't stopped. A man in Edmonton told me that that's when you really have to worry."

"He was right, if they're war drums. I think these have more to do with the eclipse. It's a mysterious event to them. Besides, why were they so friendly today if they have bad things in store for us? They can be cunning and sly but it's not like them to be two-faced. 'Two-tongued,' as they would call it."

"Well, Quinn said he would give them food and now he's making them wait. If they're being two-tongued, maybe they learned it from him."

Cameron looked pensive. "I think you're right," he said. "I wish to hell he'd lose that stubborn streak and leave. The man has no sense of anything but himself. It's him and the government the Indians are angry with, not the Company or private traders like George and you. We give them what they want, and they can live the way they've always lived. I won't deny that we overcharge them from time to time but we always make sure we do what we say we're going to do. Sometimes even a little more, and they like that. They understand that we're only here to make a profit, not to change the way they live. But the government is just the opposite. It makes a promise one day and breaks it the next, and then adds insult to injury by demanding that the Indians do things they don't really want to do. And giving them handout after handout will only hurt them in the long run, never mind the effect it has on our profit margin." Cameron paused long enough to down his drink. He burped. "Well, that's my opinion, anyway. If it sounds like a tirade, you can chalk it up to a lack of sleep."

He poured us a second drink and said. "Your original reason for coming to the Territories was to fight the Indians. What do you think of that now?"

I scarcely knew who that boy was, except that he'd read too many dime westerns. But I didn't tell that to Cameron. I said only, "It was an easy thing to say back on the coast. It's not so easy now. And it isn't because it might be staring me in the face. There are other reasons."

"Yes," Cameron said, "I can tell. But you may have to let those reasons go, Jack, if worse comes to worst. No one would think any less of you for it, least of all Big Bear. More than most people, he would know that sometimes sides have to be taken."

Big Bear. The name wormed its way through my mind. Mistahi-maskwa. Ne-moo-soom. Grandfather. All of which did nothing to lighten the load weighing so heavily on me. I had far too much respect for the old chief to want to cause him displeasure or to feel his resentment.

We talked long into the night, Cameron pouring us a third brandy, while the drums continued as a backdrop to our conversation. Instead of worrying about what the Indians might or might not do, we spoke of the coming year and the positive changes that were expected for the community, how they would benefit all of us, whites and Indians alike. It was a subject near and dear to Cameron's heart and he droned on until his voice turned into a buzz that sounded as far off as the drums. The brandy finally caught up with me and I dozed off.

I awoke with a fright. I don't know how long I'd been asleep but the ashen light of dawn was seeping into the room, the lamp guttering low. It was cold. I saw a man at Cameron's side, shaking him awake. It took only a second to grasp that he was an Indian. He spoke in Cree and I understood his short, clipped words.

"Get up!" he urged. "I think it will be a bad day today!"

NINE

Indian Fighter

IT WAS WALKING HORSE, a Woods Cree who sometimes worked for the Company. Even in the half light I could see that he was trembling.

"Big Bear's warriors have taken all the horses from the government stables! Wandering Spirit has gone to Quinn's house and taken him!"

Both Cameron and I leaped to our feet instantly and charged to the door and outside, leaving Walking Horse in our wake. Using the handrails for support we descended the slippery stairs two at a time and had no sooner rounded the corner of the building than we ran headlong into Little Bad Man and several others of his band. All of them had their faces painted with daubs of yellow ochre on their cheeks and foreheads. They were hideous. And they all carried rifles. My bowels went watery.

"I want ammunition," Little Bad Man demanded. "Do you have any?"

"Yes," Cameron said, his voice calm.

"Then give it to us."

"I can't. Not without an order from Mr. Quinn."

I hoped Cameron knew what he was doing, pushing it like that, because Little Bad Man's face turned mean. He lifted his rifle and waved it back and forth between us. "This is my order," he shouted angrily. He avoided using Cameron's Indian name.

"I'll get the key," said Cameron.

"You stay here," Little Bad Man snarled. He pointed at me. "You get it!"

I wasn't about to make him repeat himself. I spun on my heels, dashed around behind the store and back up the stairs to Cameron's room. I was inside before I realized I had no idea where the key was kept. Walking Horse was still there, sitting on Cameron's bed, afraid to come out. He said that he wasn't going anywhere until the warriors weren't able to see him leave. I thought it a good idea; they might consider him a traitor because he had warned us. He had no idea where the key was either but I reasoned Cameron wouldn't put it in too conspicuous a place because he never locked his room. I found it in the first place I looked—the top drawer of a small chest.

I returned to the store and gave Cameron the key. He opened the door, his hand steady as he inserted the key into the lock. Someone else might have stood aside and let the Indians enter first and have their way, but not Cameron. He led on his own time. Once inside, he went behind the counter and pointed to the small supply of powder and bullets. Little Bad Man stayed on the customer side and eyed him suspiciously. "Is that all you have?"

"Yes. There's more on order but it hasn't arrived yet." Cameron told the lie smoothly, without a hint of subterfuge.

Little Bad Man liked Cameron and trusted him, because he was with the Company and not the government, so he did not belabour the point. What was there was better than nothing. He and his warriors seized it all, then helped themselves to several knives from behind the counter.

Just then another Indian burst through the front door. He said to Little Bad Man that Wandering Spirit was over at the farm instructor's house with all of the whites as prisoners. Cameron and I were to be taken there immediately.

Before leaving, Cameron insisted on locking the door and Little Bad Man didn't object. It was about 200 yards to the Delaneys' house and we passed several more Indians on the way, some watching us intently. Over by the police barracks more were dancing. All were armed. The morning was clear and balmy; the sun sat on the horizon as red as blood.

The Delaney house was packed, mostly with Indians, but every white living in the village was there as well. Besides Delaney and Theresa, there were John and Mary Gowanlock, Bill Gilchrist, John Williscraft, the two priests, George Dill and Tom Quinn. There was also a handful of country-born folk that I recognized, among them John Pritchard, the interpreter, Charlie Gouin, the agency's carpenter, and Louis Goulet, a Métis who was camped at nearby Moose Creek cutting and squaring timber under a government contract.

He had come to the village simply to see what was going on and was now a prisoner like the rest of us.

I looked for Big Bear but he was nowhere to be seen. Wandering Spirit was in charge and that didn't augur well for any of us. He was the most frightening Indian I'd ever seen. Tall and lithe, he wore a beaver-skin coat with buckskin leggings under a breechclout, and a lynx-skin hat adorned with eagle feathers. Horizontal streaks of ochre running across his eyes and his mouth made his cruel face even more menacing. His bronze skin gleamed with perspiration and a fire burned in his black diamond eyes hot enough to melt steel. Those long ringlets of hair that cascaded down to his shoulders added to his nightmarish appearance. He leaned into Quinn, who was sitting, and shook a fist at him.

"Tell me who the leader of the whites is in this country? Is it the governor or the Hudson's Bay Company?"

Quinn must have thought the question silly because he laughed. "The chief of all the white men is Sir John Macdonald. He lives far away, in a place called Ottawa."

"Then you will tell him that we want beef," demanded Wandering Spirit. "And we want it right now!"

"If we had a telegraph we could send him a message that he might get right away. But we don't. We would have to go to Fort Pitt and send the message from there. That takes time. Not only that, Mr. Macdonald is a very busy man."

"You always ask us for time when we have little of it!" said the war chief. "Our people are hungry. You either give us an ox right now or we will take them all!"

Quinn sat motionless, without saying a word. You could

almost hear him thinking. He asked John Delaney, "Is there an ox in the village they can slaughter?"

"There's an old one," said Delaney, visibly relieved that Quinn was giving in to the demands. "It isn't much use to anyone anymore and might as well be eaten."

Wandering Spirit sent Pritchard and an Indian to fetch the animal. The tension in the room eased. There had been little movement till that point but now people shifted in their chairs, changed their stance if they were standing, and coughed. The air was stale and stifling, and it was plain the war chief did not like it. He let us go outside and when the priests asked, gave them permission to go to the church to prepare a service for Holy Thursday. He allowed the rest of us to follow, Catholics, Protestants, agnostics and atheists alike. It seemed like it might be the safest place in the settlement.

Two Indians ordered Cameron to accompany them back to the Company store to get tobacco. At that point Dill joined us, brought by one of Big Bear's men. He seemed in a bit of a daze and I asked if the Indians had taken anything from our store. He nodded vigorously. "They took every bloody thing," he said. "They even ransacked our room and took our guns. And the worst thing is, they took all my whisky and a couple of cases of Perry Davis Pain Killer."

Dill liked his whisky and kept a small cask on hand so that he could enjoy a drink or two before retiring. That it was now in the hands of the Indians was the most frightful news. Just as bad was the case of the painkiller they'd taken; it was part alcohol and part opium.

Cameron arrived at the church and said that Big Bear had

come to the store and ordered his braves not to touch anything. How long that would last Cameron couldn't say.
Meanwhile, the priests had donned their vestments and taken
their place at the altar. Only half of the tiny church's pews
were occupied and everyone sat close together, as if there was
safety in touching each other. Before saying mass, Father
Fafard advised us to have courage and to pray for a favourable
end to the events that were now under way in the settlement.
He had just begun the service when the sound of gunfire and
war whoops erupted outside. There were gasps of shock all
around and someone moaned, "Oh, no!"

Tom Quinn stood up as if he were about to go out and see
what was happening when the church door banged open and
Wandering Spirit burst in. He carried a Winchester rifle in his
right hand and looked like some form of devil come to take us
all to Hell. When he passed by me, I had an urge to charge him
from behind and take his weapon. I thought better of it,
though. It would have been a foolish move, as it would have
given us only one gun against many.

As we would learn later, Big Bear had indeed lost control
of his warriors, and this became even more evident when
several more Indians came storming in, indisputably drunk,
all brandishing weapons and howling like demons. I've never
been able to understand why, but Wandering Spirit strode to
the front of the church and knelt, as if he expected to receive
benediction. Was it mockery? Fear of the white man's god?
Respect? Whatever the case, as quickly as he knelt, he arose
and left the church, his eyes wide and wild, firing his rifle into
the ceiling. My ears rang from the thunderous sound in the

small building as his warriors followed him out, whooping and yipping.

Father Marchand shut the door behind them and stayed at the entrance. Father Fafard picked up the service where he had left off but was interrupted again, this time by drunken Indians in bizarre costumes of clothes and underclothes stolen from the stores. One man wore a pair of bloomers on his head, which might have been hilarious in different circumstances but in this instance it was terrifying. The interruptions became so frequent and were so noisy that Father Fafard found it pointless to continue. He ended the service, not with a prayer but with these words, "Be calm."

Wandering Spirit re-entered and ordered the congregation outside. *He's afraid to shoot us in a spiritually powerful place like a church,* I thought, *so he's going to do it outside.* We filed out, nervous as cats, not knowing what to expect but hoping for the best. Fafard and Louis Goulet lagged behind in conversation. Little Bear, one of Big Bear's councillors, belligerent and drunk, ordered the two men to catch up with the rest of us.

"I am just going to lock up," Fafard said,

Little Bear swung the butt of his rifle up and banged the priest beneath the eye. Fafard reeled back, blood flowing from a deep gash. Goulet made as if to jump the Indian but instantly found the other end of the rifle pointed at his chest. He backed off.

An old man named Yellow Bear came and got Cameron and the two of them, along with a larger group of Indians, headed in the direction of the Company store. I hoped he would be all right. As they went off, Wandering Spirit separated the whites from the rest of the congregation and he and several other Indians began to herd us down the road, past the Delaney house and Dill's store. The air was thick with gunsmoke. The war chief said that he was taking us back to Big Bear's camp as his prisoners. I looked for ways of escape but the Indians were everywhere, armed with rifles and fortified with liquor. A few were on horseback, riding in circles and firing into the air. Escape was impossible.

We had just passed the path leading to the Delaney house when Quinn stopped dead in his tracks. Not knowing what was happening, the rest of us stopped too. The agent glared at Wandering Spirit and growled, "Enough! I'm not going to anyone's camp. I'm going back to my office and you can do whatever you bloody well want to about it!"

The war chief was riled. "You are a stubborn man, Sioux Speaker! But if you like living, you will do as you are told!"

Quinn remained obdurate. "You can't tell me to do anything!"

It was as if he wanted to force a showdown, for he made no effort to leave. Wandering Spirit levered a bullet into the chamber of his Winchester. "You have a hard head, and I wonder if there is anything in it." He raised the weapon and shot Quinn through a head not so hard that a bullet couldn't split it open, and not so empty that its contents couldn't splatter on those of us standing nearby.

The women screamed; the rest of us froze, stunned by the horror of what we'd just witnessed. Charlie Gouin, whom the Indians had not bothered much because he was country-born, came to Quinn's aid. Bad Arrow, a young brave who had always been friendly to me, shot Gouin. The bullet struck his right shoulder and spun him around before he collapsed. Still alive, he tried to get up, his eyes wide with fear and a plea for his life. Miserable Man put a bullet in his chest. Gouin flopped to the ground, his entire body shaking grotesquely. He moaned for a few seconds, then died.

The killings drove the other Indians into a frenzy of whooping and rifle firing. Events were now moving so fast and were so abhorrent that I could scarcely keep track of them. My mind was in chaos, my ears ringing from the sound of the bullets. Yet I heard Big Bear's resonant voice crying for the shooting to stop. "*Tesqua! Tesqua!*" But it did not stop. Bullets kept flying through the air, punctuating the terrifying war cries. Numb with shock and fear, those of us left were prodded with rifle barrels in the direction of the camp.

I was walking beside Mary Gowanlock who was clutching her husband's left arm with both hands. The Delaneys were in front of us, their arms around each other's waists. Ahead of them were Williscraft, Gilchrist and Dill. The priests were behind us. Mary was sobbing and John was trying to comfort her, telling her that everything would be all right, when there was a "splat" sound, like a mallet striking a side of raw beef, and Gowanlock fell to his knees, the back of his neck a bloody mess. Mary went down with her husband and ended up on top of him. "John!" she cried. "Oh, John!" She grabbed hold of him, with all of her strength it seemed, as if that would prevent him from ever leaving her. A warrior I didn't recognize stuck his rifle into her back and ordered her up. Frightened out of her wits, Mary scrambled to her feet. Bill Gilchrist and I grabbed her and held her between us and we moved on.

"It's okay, Mary. It's okay," I said. She was sobbing hysterically and having trouble breathing. My mind was churning madly. We hadn't taken more than a few steps when John Delaney cried, "I'm shot!" He reeled several feet away, like a drunkard, then staggered back and collapsed at Theresa's feet.

"Oh, my God!" Theresa cried. "Father! Father!"

She was calling for one of the priests; Father Fafard came running to her side and dropped to his knees. Delaney lived only long enough to hear the priest administer consolation and say, "You are safe with God, my brother."

Those words had just passed Fafard's lips when Man Who Speaks Another Tongue shot him in the face. He fell across Delaney's corpse. Father Marchand came to the assistance of his colleague and Wandering Spirit shot him. It was as if a giant had punched the priest in the belly and knocked the wind out of him. The last words to escape his lips as he fell were, "Mon Dieu!" He lay on the path, still breathing, and Walking The Sky, a youth Fafard had raised, placed his rifle tip against the priest's head and blew it apart.

John Williscraft bolted and was shot down by Man Who Speaks Another Tongue before he had gone 10 paces. Bad Arrow and another warrior grabbed Theresa and Mary and pulled them off to the side, and it appeared as if they were pulling them away from the maelstrom of bullets. Afraid of taking one themselves, our guards scattered. Wandering Spirit screamed, "Kill all the whites!" Those of us remaining, Gilchrist, Dill and myself, ran for our lives down the trail of melting snow in the direction of the camp, simply because we couldn't see any Indians that way.

I felt the wind of a bullet and heard its zing as it whipped by my ear, and expected to catch one in my back at any second. Not far ahead, at a slight bend in the trail, there was a large clump of bushes and I thought that if I could make it to that point I could cut behind it and reach the relative safety of the woods. I heard a bullet hit Gilchrist, heard him moan as he went tumbling on his face in the muddy snow. Dill stopped and turned around, as if he was going to surrender, and I heard him cry out in pain. I turned beyond the bushes and tore into the trees, the lower branches slashing at my face.

I ran with complete disregard for roots and fallen branches, ran with only one goal in mind: to get as far away as possible from that awful Hell of raining bullets and blood and gore and death. I came out into a meadow and crossed it, too terrified to look back to see if anybody was chasing me. I entered more woods and crossed more empty meadows, up and down the gently sloping terrain, and didn't stop until I had no breath left. I collapsed in a copse of spruce and poplars, sobbing, trying to catch my breath, tears mingling with the sweat on my cheeks. I was covered in muck and soaked to the skin. I hid there like a hunted animal run to ground. Wild Jack Strong, Indian fighter.

TEN

The Scout

MY PANICKED FLIGHT HAD taken me due east of the settlement and when I had recovered my senses enough, I bore off to the southeast. I had to get to Fort Pitt, to tell Inspector Dickens of the shocking events. I considered going to the post at Onion Lake but it was also on a reserve and it was possible that disaster had struck there as well. So I continued on, knowing that it was impossible to get lost as I would eventually either intersect the main trail from Onion Lake to Fort Pitt or reach the North Saskatchewan River, which would also lead me to my destination.

It had turned into a warm spring day but there was still plenty of snow around. In many of the shallow valleys the marshes and ponds remained frozen over but were slushy and sloppy. I skirted them because I feared breaking through the ice. It added unwanted mileage to my journey but I was at least moving farther away from Frog Lake and that's all that mattered. I trudged on throughout the day and into the night, until I was too exhausted to go another step. I had no way of knowing but I calculated that I might have covered about 20 miles as the crow flies. I sought protection in a grove of trees and pulled my knees up against my chest for warmth. I never thought the wilderness could feel so safe to a solitary man. The stars that I could see through the naked branches of the trees were the same ones I'd seen at home but in different positions. I knew them better now, thanks to Cameron. I had learned so much from him and felt a need to thank him. Surely the Indians wouldn't have killed such a good man. But they were drunk on liquor and high on painkiller, and capable of anything.

I fell asleep almost immediately, despite my anguish, and woke up cold and stiff. I had no idea how long I'd slept but a full moon was just above the horizon, its pale light glistening on the snowy patches. I got up and moved around to restore some warmth to my bones. I'd had about all the sleep I was going to get and decided to move on once the moon was a little higher in the sky and I could see where I was stepping. I began to feel hungry, and to get my mind off food and the murders I tried to think pleasant thoughts, all of which escaped me. I read the constellations as Cameron had taught me, but my star-gazing ended abruptly at the Big Dipper. Its other name was Ursa Major or Big Bear. The events of the morning intruded like bullies and dominated every corner of my mind. I could not believe that so many of my friends were dead and I was alive. It was difficult to keep from crying and more than once I didn't bother trying. I worried about Theresa and Mary. Did Bad Arrow and his friend have their welfare in mind when they pulled them from danger? Or did they have other, more sinister motives? Did my fleeing leave them to die? I both craved and feared the answers.

I waited until the moon was up several degrees and, using it as a guide, started walking again. Still not completely sure of my footing, I moved slowly. I had gone only a few hundred yards when I came upon the Onion Lake–Fort Pitt trail. I was no expert at reading tracks but it looked as though a wagon had been on the trail recently. Exactly how long ago I couldn't say, but the ruts seemed fresh. Farther along, horse droppings confirmed my suspicions. The wagon must have passed while I was sleeping.

I recognized the part of the trail I was on—it curved in a broad arc to the northwest and Onion Lake—and knew that I wasn't more than a mile or two from the settlement there and perhaps 10 miles from the fort. Had I known it was so close I could have already been there, in warm, dry clothes and with food in my belly. Provided, of course, that the fort had not been sacked by Indians.

I hurried along, able to move swiftly now, and at full light stood on the low ridge overlooking Fort Pitt. It was still intact and there were no Indians about. Smoke drifted skyward from chimneys and people moved among the buildings. It was all very peaceful and normal. I ran down the slope to the sanctuary awaiting me there.

William McLean and Inspector Dickens scarcely knew who I was at first because I was so filthy, but then greeted me as if

I had returned from the grave. McLean gave me a change of clothes while his wife took mine to wash. Mrs. McLean brought me a bowl of porridge and some bacon and I wolfed it down like a starving animal.

Everyone knew of the massacre well before my arrival, even to the number of people killed. They had also heard that Cameron was still alive but a captive of the Indians. Apparently, some friendly Woods Cree had gone to the post at Onion Lake and told George Mann, the farming instructor there, about the events at Frog Lake. They warned him that if he valued his life and that of his family, he would take them and leave immediately for Fort Pitt. Mann did exactly that but other Indians had the road blocked, forcing him to manoeuvre his buckboard through a snowy swamp. He got lost and had to wait until the moon rose to get his bearings. Sitting there in the cold and dark he could hear the marauding Indians whooping and firing their guns as they looted his home and the warehouse. He and his family arrived at the fort at one o'clock in the morning. It was their buckboard that had passed within a few hundred yards of where I slept.

In McLean's office, the factor and Dickens pumped me for more information. I gave them all the gruesome details that would be branded on my mind forever. Now that I was relatively safe, I felt guilty that I had fled like a dog, and blurted out a confession. Dickens merely nodded, unmoved by such candour, but McLean gripped my shoulder and said, "Go easy on yourself, lad. There isn't one of us here who wouldn't have done the same thing, and any man who says otherwise is either a liar or a damned fool. What's more, we need you here alive, not back at the lake dead."

His words, appreciated as they were, mollified my rampaging conscience only slightly. I looked around the room that I had been in only three months before, toasting the New Year, as full of optimism as I had ever been, and was nearly overcome by the loss. I hung my head and tears fell, silently. I did not want to cry in front of those men, but they fell nonetheless.

"You need to get some rest, lad," McLean said. "Your experience has been dearly bought."

With the Frog Lake detachment staying at the fort, there were no spare beds in the barracks for me but McLean, anticipating refugees, had turned the reception hall into makeshift quarters. I would have to sleep on the floor but it was dry, and there were plenty of blankets available. It was better than a feather mattress to me and I slept till suppertime.

I awoke famished, and more hopeful than I'd been when I went to bed. There was an aroma of roast beef wafting from the kitchen and it made my mouth water. I went in search of food and drink. Out in the hall I encountered Amelia and I was pleased when she wrapped her arms around me in a warm hug.

"I'm so sorry, Jack," she said. "What an awful time you've been through!"

I would have gladly let her hold me forever but there was a commotion outside and shouts of warnings, and the two of us ran out the door to see what was happening. McLean was there and so was Dickens. And up on the ridge stood several Indians.

Their gestures indicated that they wanted a meeting and

they motioned for the factor to come up to the ridge. McLean suggested that Dickens ought to go with him.

"Ah, n-n-no, Bill," Dickens said. "It wouldn't b-b-be wise if I went, or any of m-m-my men. We r-r-represent what the Indians hate m-m-most. It's b-b-best we don't rile them any m-m-more than we already have."

I had to give McLean credit. You could see in his eyes that he believed Dickens's concern was more for his own safety than anything else and was tantamount to cowardice. But he said nothing. As his grasp of the Cree language was modest, he rounded up an interpreter to ensure that everything said was clearly understood. Together the two men walked up the hill, unarmed, to meet the Indians. They all disappeared down the far side and those of us standing below held our collective breath.

We waited anxiously but the two Company men soon bobbed up over the ridge with two other people in tow. I recognized them straight off as Charles Quinney, the Anglican minister at Onion Lake, and his wife. Cut Arm, chief of the Onion Lake reserve, had brought them down to safety. Quinney said that Cut Arm had also told him about Frog Lake and that the women and Bill Cameron were indeed still alive and being held captive. However, he couldn't say with any certainty what Big Bear's band and the Woods Cree were up to. It would be wise, though, for those of us in the fort to take every precaution.

With the further news that Cameron was all right, I was beginning to believe it might be true. It was a pinpoint of light in a black universe. I did not stay up long after supper

but went to the reception hall and slept till early the following morning.

We spent the next couple of days dismantling all of the
outbuildings and anything else that might serve to conceal an
Indian. As there was no stockade, we used this wood, as well
as logs and firewood, to build walls between the six buildings
that comprised the fort. Where the fort faced the ridge the
gaps were much larger and these were crammed with carts and
wagons turned on their sides. We made loopholes here and
there for sentries to see and shoot through if necessary. Inside
the buildings, we piled bags of flour and oats against the windows, again leaving sentry loopholes.

McLean was not only the fort's factor but also justice of the
peace for the Territories. He insisted that every able-bodied
male civilian in the fort be sworn in as a special constable. I did
not object to it and gladly accepted the rifle given me.

Each night at sundown, everyone went inside and the
doors were barricaded till dawn. Amelia's bedroom was at
the back of the McLean house, on the second floor, and
commanded a good view of the ridge, so it became the lookout post. Blankets were strung across the room to create a
separate part for sleeping. The watches were two hours long
and even the girls, who had also been issued rifles, took
their turn, as they did at the loopholes during the day. I
shared a watch with Amelia but with others sleeping in the
room and the need to be vigilant, there was little time for
idle chatter. However, she laid her hand on my arm and
said, "I'm so glad you're safe, Jack."

I showed her how to get the most out of her rifle, should

she have to use it in the dark. I moistened the sight with spit and then rubbed it with the phosphorous head of a match so that it glowed. It was a little trick that Cameron had taught me, and she was duly impressed. To my mind, she was conducting herself admirably in the face of such grave danger and of the two of us, I was the more nervous. But then, she had not seen what I'd seen.

One night there was a severe snowstorm, the last of the season, I hoped, although those with experience in the country had developed a healthy degree of scepticism. The wind blew and the snow swirled into shapes that the sentries thought were Indians and we had more false alarms that night than any other. The following day burst forth warm and sunny. During the afternoon, Indians appeared on the benches across the river.

It was Little Poplar and his band. He sent word that he wanted food for himself and his people, so McLean, out of compassion rather than fear, gave them some, despite Dickens's objections. Meanwhile, he had a bastion built between the fort and the river as added protection.

More than a week had passed and there were no signs of Indians on our northern and most vulnerable flank. Because the weather had remained fine and the snow was almost gone, Dickens decided to send some scouts up to Frog Lake to try to locate Big Bear and his band. He assigned Larry Loasby, who had been a member of the Frog Lake detachment, along with one of his own men, Corporal Dave Cowan, a humourless man with an abbreviated moustache. Because of my familiarity with the settlement, Dickens asked if I was interested in going.

My heart was in my throat when I said yes but I could not

say no. We were to ride up the trail that parallelled the river to Frog Creek, then follow the creek to the settlement. If we found nothing, we were to return via Onion Lake. With any luck at all we would find that the Indians had either not moved or had taken the Fort Carlton trail to join Riel. In either case, it would mean that Fort Pitt was safe, at least for a while. The inspector cautioned us that we were a scouting party, not a war party, and to avoid an encounter with the Indians at all costs. I said nothing but I knew that if the slightest opportunity arose to rescue Cameron, I was going to take full advantage of it.

When McLean heard about the assignment, he was livid. "Frank," he said to Dickens, "at best you're lessening the fort's strength and at worst you're sending these men to their deaths and giving the Indians three more guns and three good horses."

Dickens was not about to have his authority questioned by a civilian. "W-w-we are only as s-s-safe as the intelligence we have p-p-permits. We have n-n-none, and desperately n-n-need it. These m-m-men will g-g-go."

Though I appreciated McLean's concern, I was squarely on Dickens's side this time. We were completely in the dark about what the Indians were up to, and needed information.

Cowan, Loasby and I were given the three best horses in the stable. We saddled them, taking bedrolls, saddle bags with enough food for two days, and scabbards for our rifles. As I climbed on my horse and felt its power between my legs, felt it travel upward and into me, I was ready for anything.

"God speed," McLean said as we spurred our animals out

of the corral and picked up the trail along the river. The air was mild, the sky grey; the clouds seemed high and held no threat of rain.

We moved as quickly as the terrain would allow but it was soggy with snow and mud, and many of the coulees were steep-sided and slippery, further hindering our progress. Most of the ice on the river had broken up and was now drifting in large chunks with the current. We reached Frog Creek more quickly than I thought we would, perhaps because I was in no hurry to get there.

We could smell the buildings at the Gowanlocks' place before we saw them, the unmistakeable odour of wet, burned wood carried on the soft breeze. From the edge of a thicket, we could see that both mills and the house were charred skeletons. I was heartsick. A lot of sweat and hope had gone into those buildings, mine included, and I despaired to see them end up as ash. We couldn't see any signs of life but waited for a few minutes anyway, just to make sure. Nothing moved and the only sound was the occasional gentle murmuring of the wind in the trees.

"It looks clear," Cowan said and we urged our horses toward the ruins, one hand on the reins, the other holding our rifles. I laid mine across the pommel of my saddle. We rode single file, with Cowan leading and Loasby bringing up the rear. The horses were nervous passing the rubble, as unsettled by the smell as I was by the sight. The only sounds now were the animals' breathing and their hooves striking the soft earth.

As we approached the site of Big Bear's camp, we heard

dogs barking, which meant the band hadn't packed up and left; at least not all of them. We threaded our way among the trees east of the camp to a point that offered a suitable view through Cowan's field glasses. Most of the lodges were still there but only old men, women and small children occupied them. Big Bear and his warriors were gone.

We stayed deep in the trees and gave the camp a wide berth, just in case there were a few warriors left, but I was willing to bet there weren't. And if they'd gone anywhere, it was more than likely Fort Pitt. Had they intended on going 200 miles east to join Riel, I believed they would have moved the entire camp. I said as much to the policemen.

"We'll see," said Cowan. "Let's hope you're wrong."

We continued north, moving as quietly as possible, only half-prepared for what awaited us. The settlement was an eerie, ghastly sight. Not only had all of the buildings been burned but most of the bodies still lay exactly as they had fallen. They were grotesque caricatures of the men I once knew, but easily identifiable by their hair colour and clothes, and by the fact that I knew where they had been killed. The memory of that morning came flooding back so vividly that my heart seemed to be missing every second beat and my stomach was in turmoil.

We passed the bush I had run behind and came upon Dill first, then Gilchrist only paces away. Off to the side of the trail was Williscraft. Farther along, near the path to the Delaney house, were the bodies of Quinn and Gouin. Quinn, with a willow stick stuck in his chest, was now propped up against a tree in a sitting position, with a pipe jammed in his mouth. Strangely, the bodies of the two priests, Delaney and Gowanlock were nowhere to be seen.

Someone had gone to the trouble of removing them and I wondered why they had taken only four of the bodies and not the others. It's possible that the half-breeds, many of whom were Roman Catholic, had buried Fathers Fafard and Marchand, but why Delaney and Gowanlock? We searched for markers but saw none. Upon reaching the blackened ruins of the church, we discovered why. There, in its stone basement, now exposed, were four charred corpses. It was impossible to tell who was who. Cowan groaned and Loasby, a Catholic, crossed himself. Both men had turned pale but didn't say anything. My stomach started to heave again. I dismounted, bent over beside my horse and deposited my lunch on the ground. I wanted to run, to leave this awful place far behind, to go back to the coast where some semblance of sanity existed. It was all I could do just to climb back on my horse. "Let's get out of here," I growled.

We could see by the tracks leading from the settlement to the east that a large number of horses had left the area. Even so, we went to investigate the Woods Cree camp; its numbers also reflected the absence of warriors.

It was getting dark and we were all tired and stiff from the long day's ride. We steered the horses well east of the lake and off the trail, and camped for the night behind a curtain of trees. My stomach still felt upset and I was so emotionally drained that I had no appetite for food when my companions ate. Few words passed among us as we sat around the small fire, and we all turned in early. When at last I fell asleep I dreamed of hideously deformed bodies that beckoned me to come join them. I awoke in a sweat, trembling from head to toe, threw more wood on the fire and lay there, huddled in my blanket, wide awake, until the dawn cracked the night sky. I slept then, for only moments, it seemed, before Cowan shook me awake.

"Time to get moving, Jack," he said. Both he and Loasby looked as if they hadn't slept much either.

We breakfasted on jerky, eating out of necessity more than hunger. We talked out of necessity, too, with little desire for casual conversation. Cowan and Loasby were dealing with their own emotions and hadn't really said much since the settlement. Loasby had known every one of those men lying dead beside the trail and in the church basement, Cowan most of them, and I could sense both men's anger. But it wasn't anger I felt as much as a dispiriting sadness. For the lucky ones, the innocence of the world bids a long farewell, but for me it had disappeared in a trice, like some trick of magic.

The wind had picked up overnight and was blowing wild and icy. The sky was a dull overcast, a wintry day, when yesterday had held the promise of spring. We rejoined the trail and went to Onion Lake where we found more burned buildings and no warriors in the Indian encampment. Chief Cut Arm had apparently joined up with Big Bear and they had moved south together, in the direction of Fort Pitt.

The trail was badly churned up by both shod and unshod ponies, which indicated that the Indians were riding several stolen government animals. And if their tracks didn't veer to the east soon—an unrealistic expectation—we could count on finding them near or at Fort Pitt. The positive side to it was that Big Bear would not be expecting us to be scouting him from the rear, which gave us a distinct advantage. Somehow, though, we would have to find a way around him in order to get home. It began to snow heavily and the wind remained stiff.

We weren't much more than a mile from the fort when we spotted smoke from their lodges. They were camped this side of the ridge above the fort, but well off the trail to the east, at the edge of a dense poplar forest. To our right, or the west side of the trail, the poplar forest was equally dense and would be near impossible to ride through. We hid in a thicket and discussed our options.

We could wait until dark and try to sneak by the camp, but we didn't think it would be possible without disturbing the dogs. We could sneak up part of the way and gallop the rest but the trail was treacherous enough during the day at full speed, let alone at night. We considered leaving the horses and circling around through the trees on foot but Cowan didn't want to leave three perfectly good animals for the enemy. Dickens wouldn't like having to account to his superiors for them, nor would he appreciate the loss of face with McLean, who had predicted it. Our fourth choice was bold, yet the more we talked about it the more Cowan believed we could pull it off. We would wait till dusk, when there was still enough light to see the road, wrap our blankets around our shoulders, which would hide Cowan's and Loasby's uniforms, and ride casually toward the camp as if we belonged there. If we were spotted, we might be taken for Indians or half-breeds in the poor visibility. With any luck at all we might get part of the way through the camp before we had to gallop. Then we'd just have to hope that the element of surprise would see us safely over the ridge.

Cowan said, "Big Bear won't be expecting anyone from this direction and by the time he realizes who it is, we ought to stand a good chance of making the ridge. We're downwind, so that should hide the sound of our approach. Once we're spotted, ride like hell. It's not easy to hit a moving target, especially in this weather, and we should be all right as long as we don't bunch up. Whatever you do, don't stop for anything, even if one of us goes down. That's an order."

I could see that Loasby had reservations but he didn't say anything. Ultimately, it didn't matter what Loasby or I thought: Cowan was the NCO in charge and he was calling the shots.

I don't know how long we waited but it didn't seem long enough. With our knives, we dug through the snow and into the soil, smearing our hands and faces with it. The two policemen removed their telltale pillbox hats and I wished we had feathers to replace them. It would have further improved our disguise.

We mounted our horses and wrapped ourselves in the blankets.

"Ready?" Cowan asked.

Loasby and I nodded. *Ready, but hardly willing,* I thought.

We moved out slowly, in single file, heads down but never taking our eyes off the camp for a second. My horse whickered, which I expected one of them to do when they got their first whiff of the camp, but the gusting wind hid it. We were almost to the edge of the camp before they saw us. At first there was confusion over who we might be, then someone cried, "*Chemoginusuk!*" Police! I spurred my horse into a gallop and let go of my blanket, which went flying off in the wind. I saw Cowan's fly too, as he took the reins with both hands. I heard Loasby curse and knew he was right behind me. We were half-way past the camp before the Indians got a shot off. Then there was a burst of gunfire and everything became sharply defined, like an etching in black and white.

We only had about a hundred yards to cover to reach the brow of the ridge and safety when, ahead of me, a bullet caught Cowan's horse. It came to an abrupt halt that threw him off balance. The last I saw of him he had one leg over the saddle and both arms around the animal's neck, hanging on for dear life. I knew he was in desperate straits but I was having troubles of my own. Trying to avoid Cowan, my horse veered toward the forest, stumbled and went down with a painful grunt, the wind knocked out of it. I flew arse over head into the trees and was lucky not to break anything. I scrambled to my feet, looked back once to see Loasby knocked from his horse by a bullet at the top of the ridge, and ran for my life again.

Although I could hear more gunfire, it seemed to be coming from the other side of the ridge. I didn't know what to make of it, but nobody was chasing me and for that I was thankful. They probably had Cowan and Loasby as prizes, if the pair weren't already dead. I ran, and the only thing I can say for myself is that I was nowhere near as panic-stricken as I was at Frog Lake.

I continued west, through the densely wooded valley. I

knew that the river was somewhere off to my left but it would be a dead end and I wanted to put as much distance as possible between myself and the Indians before turning toward it, just in case they had decided to come after me. I threaded a path through closely packed trees, the underbrush snagging my clothes and whipping my face. I stopped to listen but could hear nothing beyond my breathing and the pounding of my heart. The snow on fallen branches made the footing slippery and treacherous, so I slowed my pace; I didn't want to risk a sprained or broken ankle in this wilderness. I don't know how far I'd gone when I came to a bush-filled coulee that I knew must lead to the river. I turned down it, the wind still fierce and the snow heavy. I was certain that I was heading in the right direction but with the blowing snow and limited visibility, I couldn't be certain. It began to get dark, so I found a small depression among some willows, out of the wind, and with numb fingers lit a fire. With any luck at all, the storm would blow itself out overnight.

Even with the fire I was frozen to the core without my blanket, and I was ravenous. The wind howled and blew snow in every direction. I doubted that the Indians would be hunting me in it and would have lost my trail if they were. It was well past midnight when the storm began to abate and the sky to clear, enough to allow me to get my bearings. As soon as I was able to confirm that I was on the right track I put the North Star at my back and continued down the coulee, glad to be on the move again and building body heat, although my clothes were damp and clammy. I reached the river in less time than I figured it would take and made my way downstream, along the path the Mounties and I had travelled two days before. I must have run a long way into the bush escaping from the Indians because it was some time before I was in sight of the fort.

Everything seemed just as it had been when I left, complete with the barricades, which I took as a favourable sign. I waited, crouched and shivering behind some bushes until it was fully light. I didn't want a sentry to mistake me for an Indian in the dark and blow my head off. When I deemed it safe, I ran toward the barricade shouting, "Hello the fort! Hello the fort! It's Jack Strong! Hello the fort!"

Up at one of the windows, I saw the vague outline of a face peering out at me. Was it Amelia? I began to wave and the face pressed closer to the glass.

It was Wandering Spirit.

ELEVEN

Prisoner

I COULD HEAR CRIES OF ALARM coming from the fort and knew that the Indians would be on my tail in seconds. I ran down to the river, retracing my footsteps. Without any clear plan as to what I should do, but knowing that this time I couldn't outrun them, I acted on instinct alone. When I didn't see anyone behind me, I leaped over the bank, landing a dozen feet or so below the edge. To my immediate left there was an overhang with a hole beneath it. I quickly smoothed over the snow where I had landed, as best I could, then crawled headfirst into the hole. Since I didn't leave any tracks going over the bank I hoped that the Indians wouldn't be able to see where I had landed and would give up looking for me. They had vivid imaginations and could easily believe that I had vanished into thin air. That was the kind of wild card I needed to get away with this stunt, but I had a sinking feeling that I was about to be trumped.

I heard voices on the trail above. It sounded like two men and one of them said that he was certain I was unarmed. I recognized the voice but I couldn't pinpoint it. When the other voice responded, silky and smooth, I knew instantly that it belonged to Wandering Spirit.

There's a soft sound that moccasins make in the snow that is markedly different from heavy leather boots and that's what I heard coming down the slope toward my hiding place. They stopped. I held my breath and could hear someone else breathing. I was sure I'd been found but didn't want to make the first move in case I was wrong. I was also afraid. Nothing happened for a few seconds and I thought perhaps my pursuer had missed me. Then something nudged my boots and the voice I had first recognized said, "Come on out, Jack. Quickly!"

It sounded like my salvation and I wasted no time crawling out, feeling as foolish as I was scared. Standing above me was Isidore Mondion, tall and moustachioed, and one of the Woods Cree councillors from Frog Lake with whom I'd had tea on occasion. The look on his face suggested he thought that I was even more of a fool than I felt.

Just then Wandering Spirit appeared at the top of the slope, his face cruel with hatred. He raised his rifle and aimed it at me. *I'm dead,* I thought, but Mondion sprang in front as a shield.

"*Tesqua!* He is my little brother and my life is his. You will not harm him!"

Wandering Spirit snarled like an animal denied its prey, but lowered his weapon. Mondion was his equal and he could do nothing about it, yet he was clearly out for blood. My blood.

"As you wish, Neestas. But if you value your brother's life you will see that he does not run again."

I had protection, at least for a while.

On the way back to the fort, Mondion put his arm around me and told me that he had been momentarily confused when my tracks suddenly disappeared. My idea might have worked if he hadn't peered over the edge of the bank and seen that the snow below had been disturbed.

"Human beings just don't disappear," he said. When he came down, he could see a small part of my boot protruding from the snow. "You are big for a burrowing animal, little brother," he added, smiling.

Burrowing animal or not, I thanked my lucky stars and Mondion that he had had the presence of mind to accompany Wandering Spirit after the war chief recognized me from the window. "I knew he would kill you if I didn't," he said.

Inside the fort, other warriors greeted me with cries of recognition, saying, "His medicine is strong! Bullets cannot pierce him!"

Bullets can't pierce a man if they don't hit him, I thought, but I kept that piece of information to myself; if they reckoned I was superhuman, I'd have been a damned fool to deny it. They could believe whatever they wanted: All I believed in was pure blind luck and mine had come close to running out for good. I was fortunate to be alive, but I was glad that Ma and Joe couldn't see me. My record as an Indian fighter was about as dismal as a west coast winter.

There were no other whites about and after a brief discussion between Mondion and some of the braves, in which he told them the same thing he had told Wandering Spirit, I was taken up to the camp. As we descended on the far side of the ridge, we passed the bloody mess that was Cowan's body, pulled off to the side of the trail. Beside him, on a pointed stick shoved into the ground, was his heart. A few feet away lay the carcass of his horse. I couldn't stomach any more and turned away. In camp, I discovered why there were no whites at the fort. They were all prisoners. All except Dickens and his men, who, I learned later, had gone to Fort Battleford.

When I encountered Big Bear he seemed to have aged a dozen years since I had last seen him, the furrows on his face deepened into canyons. If he was surprised to see me captured, he didn't show it. I knew I could be honest with him and expressed my disappointment over the turn of events. He said that he was as sickened by what had happened as I was, and openly admitted that he had lost control of his warriors once the moon had turned dark. Riel had said that if that happened, they would need to kill all the white men.

"But I did not want to fight with the whites, not even the police," he said. His eyes gleamed with moisture, yet his face showed no sign of emotion. "It is not easy for me to say, but maybe this is the only path for people who do not understand each other. Maybe we will destroy you or you will destroy us so that one of us can start all over again."

"There must be another way, Ne-moo-soom," I said.

"No matter the path, our destinies are entwined and my heart is heavy." As he turned to go, he added, "Three times you have escaped death, No-see-sim [Grandson]. Your medicine is good. Still, you should be careful."

I sought out McLean and spoke with him. He was generally an optimistic man but I could easily read the concern on his face. He filled me in on what had happened after Cowan, Loasby and I had left on the scouting trip.

"The three of you had hardly disappeared up the river trail when the Indians appeared on the ridge above the fort. There must have been more than 200 of them, all mounted. It was a terrifying sight, believe me. The first thing they did was slaughter seven or eight of the Company's oxen and take them back over the ridge. There was nothing we could do to stop them. They sent several messages to the fort, demanding things like tea, tobacco and clothes, which we gave them without arguing. I suppose we hoped that they would eventually go on their way. But they didn't, of course. Later on, Miserable Man came down and demanded a kettle to boil the tea. A lot of gall, I'd say. The last message that came was from Wandering Spirit. He said that all the civilians would be killed if the police didn't leave immediately. They had us ten to one, so Dickens didn't argue the point. The last I saw of him and his detachment they were repairing the old scow for a trip down the river to Battleford. Everyone else was brought here to the camp as prisoners."

First though, McLean had gone to the Indians' camp, again with an interpreter to be on the safe side, to see what could be sorted out. When they passed the calumet around and didn't offer it to him, the factor knew the whites were in trouble. The councillors said they were sorry for what they'd done but that they were sick and tired of their maltreatment at the hands of the white man. Big Bear insisted that it was their intent to drive the government and all whites from the land.

"Your quest is hopeless," McLean had told him. "You do not understand the power of the forces that will be brought to bear upon you. You will not survive them. It would be best for all concerned if you returned peaceably to your camp at Frog Lake and handed over the murderers to the police."

It was about then that Cowan, Loasby and I had interrupted the meeting and put an end to whatever progress he might have been making.

"Cowan was wounded badly after his horse threw him," McLean said. "We ran to help but they warned us away with guns. Louison Mongrain finished him off. Cowan put up his arms as if to ward off the bullets and begged for his life. It was heart-wrenching. I heard him say, 'Don't, brother, don't,' but Mongrain wasn't listening and shot him again. Then he cut out his heart and put it on a stick. That's supposed be a sign of respect but it's beyond my ken."

Loasby was shot off his horse and staggered to the fort with the aid of cover fire—the shots I had heard during my escape. "If he lived, he was lucky. Another 15 minutes and Dickens would have been gone. If Loasby made it to Fort Battleford he'll get better medical attention there."

McLean sighed. "I don't know why Cowan thought the three of you could get away with such a damned fool stunt. The only bright mark in the day was to see you disappearing among the trees. You should thank Providence you're still alive." He shook his head. "I just don't know what Cowan was thinking."

But I knew what he'd been thinking. He was underestimating the Indians, as many whites were prone to do, and he had paid the price for it.

"I pleaded with them to let us bury Cowan but they wouldn't allow it," Mclean said, clearly upset by the whole affair. "Then Amelia and Eliza came to see if I was all right—I swear those girls have no fear—and I sent them back. It didn't matter anyway. Shortly after you escaped into the woods the Indians overran the fort and took everyone prisoner, including my family. Dickens had already gone and I had told Helen to take the children and go with him should I not return but she would not leave me behind. None of them would."

That didn't surprise me a bit. The McLean family believed they were as much a part of this country as the poplar trees. And they were just as hardy. Later, when I saw Amelia, she was bearing up better than most people would under the circumstances.

"My father taught me never to be afraid of Indians," she said. "And I'm not." When the Indians wondered why she and her sisters weren't afraid, she said in her passable Cree, "For many years we have lived side by side as brothers and sisters. Do we not speak the same language? We have no reason to be afraid of you."

In a way she was throwing down the gauntlet to them, an attractive young woman saying, "I trust you. Now what will you do with that trust? Will you violate it? Or will you honour it?" Most reasonable human beings would honour it and that's what the Indians did. This is not to say that there weren't a few unscrupulous braves who had an eye on the McLean girls for wives and other more unthinkable uses. There were, but most of them respected her forthrightness and lack of fear, and I did too. I couldn't honestly say that I would have stayed behind had I been in her shoes.

While the Indians looted the fort, a few of the half-breeds were given the job of building a raft to bring Little Poplar and his small band across the river to join Big Bear, as we whites repaired commandeered carts and loaded them with goods stolen from the fort. We were also their servants and had to fetch water, chop wood and keep the fires going. Our captors gorged themselves on beef and anything else that suited their palates, and we shared in the surfeit of food. Not only did we get beef but we were given tins of *pâté de foie gras*, lobster, salmon, green corn and condensed milk, and any other food item the Indians considered disgusting.

At one point the residents of the fort were allowed to return to retrieve some of their personal belongings. Amelia could not resist playing one last tune on the organ, which terrified the Indians who believed the instrument hid evil spirits. They took axes and chopped it into little pieces and set fire to it. Then they burned the fort.

Three days after I had been taken captive we were told that we were going back to Frog Lake. We packed up and left without being able to bury Cowan. His body still lay sprawled beside the road, near his horse, both corpses bloated and fly-blown, his heart browning and shrivelling in the sun. Smoke and ash drifted skyward from behind the ridge. But to the Indians it was not just smoke and ash disappearing in the air; it was a symbol of a government that had failed to keep its promises.

Wandering Spirit led the way on a grey mare he had stolen from the fort and decorated with mud stripes and feathers. He rode tall and proud, like a man who had just conquered the world. The rest of the band rode horses or drove carts, but the prisoners walked, with the exception of McLean's family. He managed to finagle a cart for them, although Amelia wouldn't have anything to do with it and walked with the rest of us. The trail was mushy with mud and fast-melting snow. It was warm, though, and that was some consolation. After a false spring, it seemed as if the real thing had come to the prairies at last.

At Frog Lake I was both pleased and relieved to find that Cameron was none the worse for his two weeks in captivity, and our reunion was as happy as it could be given the conditions. More good news was finding that Mary and Theresa were also coping well with their ordeal. After the slaughter, their captors had taken them to Big Bear's camp. They expected the worst, but Louis Goulet and John Pritchard came to their rescue and bought them for two horses each. Had they not done so, the two women would have automatically become the wives of the Indians who had captured them. I saw them only briefly and from a distance. They were kept in a different part of the camp, along with the McLeans, and by necessity were still pretending to be the wives of the half-breeds. Heart-felt waves were all we managed but knowing we were all still alive was comforting.

I was surprised to learn that they and Cameron had been in the Indian camp when Cowan, Loasby and I rode by. Cameron had had plenty of opportunities to escape, as the Indians usually left him unguarded, but any attempt would have resulted in the deaths of other prisoners. I asked him about the day of the massacre.

"I tell you, Jack, I thought I was done for. When I went to the store with Yellow Bear, he asked me straight out whose side I was on, Riel's or the police. I almost said I had to be on the government's side but I thought better of it. Instead, I said neither, that it was their battle and they should fight it among themselves, and it had nothing to do with our friendship. Yellow Bear believed me. He found a red shawl and disguised me as a woman and then had two of his wives take me to Big Bear's camp. I was sandwiched between them and I couldn't stop shaking. They kept me in a lodge for a while and told me I'd be safe, but I never quite believed it. There were some individuals who wanted to kill me just because I was white." He fell silent for a while, as if he were uncertain about what to say next. "You know, Jack, I've never been able to find faith in a god. I guess I've never needed it because I've always had more than enough faith in myself. Yet it seemed to desert me. For the first time in my life I was at a loss over what to do. I felt betrayed and scared out of my wits. And even worse, I felt all alone."

Cameron was keen to know the details of my scouting trip to the settlement. He grimaced when I described the burned buildings and the other gruesome sights, even though he was aware of them.

"I knew they burned the place because I saw the smoke," he said. "And Louis Goulet told me about the bodies. We wanted to bury them but the Indians wouldn't let us. They wanted them left right where they were. Louis persuaded Big Bear to at least allow him to move them into the church, but he was

only able to get four into the basement before some warriors
came along and told him that if he wanted to live he'd stop
what he was doing. Louis wondered why they didn't want him
to move the bodies until he watched one of them open Tom
Quinn's jacket and shirt and shove a sharpened willow stick
into his chest.

"Good God!" I said, and told Bill of the sight I'd seen,
how they had heaped further indignities on Quinn's body by
sitting him up and sticking a pipe in his mouth. "They must
have really hated him to do something like that."

I could not reconcile those barbaric deeds with the gentle
people who had befriended me at Frog Lake. It made no sense
to me whatsoever. I remembered the matchbox Cameron had
once shown me, and realized that savagery, like beauty, is in
the eye of the beholder and depends on which side of the box
you've grown up on.

Two and a half weeks after the massacre, the Indians finally
permitted us to bury the bodies, and several of us went to the
settlement to complete the task. I knew what to expect and tried
to warn the others but my words could not match the reality.
The corpses had still not been moved and had grown even more
grotesque in the interim; animals had gnawed some of them
and all were swarming with flies in the warm weather. The smell
was nauseating and the only way we could handle them was to
cover them with blankets to reduce the odour and hide their
hideousness. Nonetheless, we gave them a decent burial, even
Quinn, though I had little sympathy for him. The four charred
bodies in the church were left where they lay after someone
tried to move one and pieces of burned meat came off.

The grisly task left everyone feeling out of sorts or physically ill. Yet we'd only just completed it when I was faced with another task equally appalling. An old lady had taken ill and became deranged, raving that she was becoming a *wendigo* and should be killed. Now if there's one word that will set an Indian quivering in his moccasins, it's that one. A *wendigo* is a cannibal with superhuman powers, capable of eating an entire camp. It accomplishes this by letting out a scream that paralyzes everyone within hearing, at which point it can eat at its leisure. The only way to prevent this is to kill the afflicted person, but because it is superhuman, the job requires someone with special powers.

A Catholic priest has such powers but the priests were dead and would have declined the job anyway, not being in the business of taking lives. Another option was a rifle loaded with some holy object, such as small pieces of a chalice, or something else from a church. This was the solution demanded by Big Bear. There would be an even greater chance of success if a Catholic pulled the trigger, so all the Catholic half-breeds in camp were approached. None wanted the job and begged off with a variety of lame excuses, the most common being that they would be so scared they would miss, which would only further anger the wendigo. In reality, though, they knew that once the rebellion ended and the whites got wind of the slaying, the person who did it would be charged with murder and maybe even hanged.

With no alternatives, the Bear assigned three Indians to the chore. The woman couldn't be killed in camp and since they did not want the job of moving her themselves, they forced Louis Goulet and me to do it, Louis because he was Catholic and me because of my strong medicine.

The old woman could not walk so we made a stretcher from two poles and a bearskin. Goulet called this an *apichimou*. We took it to the woman's lodge, left it outside the door and entered. She was tiny and frail, and weighed next to nothing. Wires bound her wrists and ankles and she was moaning and babbling. I could not make out her words but Goulet said she was threatening to turn into a wendigo at any moment and would eat a white man before sunset. She was begging us to kill her right away because she feared it might be me.

How anybody could be afraid of that pathetic creature was difficult to imagine and I felt bad for her, not to mention pangs of guilt about what we were doing. I said to Goulet, "I'm not sure I can do this, Louis. We're taking her to her death."

"Dat's right," he said in his thick French accent. "But den you just t'ink of de friends 'er people killed on dat 'oly T'ursday, and maybe it be easier for you."

But it wasn't.

The woman was sitting on a deerskin, so Louis grabbed one side and I the other and we carried her from the lodge and sat her on the apichimou. She neither resisted nor complained, but continued to moan and mutter words I couldn't understand. The three Indians charged with the responsibility of killing her, plus a few dozen older men, led us about a quarter mile away from camp to the base of a poplar bluff, and ordered us to set the woman down there. She was still in a sitting position and had been for the entire journey. Goulet and I moved back a respectable distance to watch the proceedings.

I knew one of the Indians about to do the killing. He was an older warrior named Dressy Man and he had smeared himself with soot and appeared more frightful and dangerous than the old woman. He held a club, while another had a rifle and the third a sabre that the police had left behind.

Dressy Man sneaked up behind the old lady and threw a shawl over her head, then with a massive swing of his weapon, brained her. She fell over on her side, her entire body shaking like aspen leaves in the wind. Immediately, the Indian with the rifle came over and shot her three times in the chest. The one with the sabre removed the shawl and sliced her head off in a single stroke. Then he grabbed the head by the braids and flung it as far from the body as possible, as wendigos have an ability to reattach themselves if the body parts remain too close together. He had tried to throw it over some willow bushes, out of sight, but it hung up on a branch instead and swung by the braids, leaking blood. I've never seen so many scared Indians in my life. They nearly trampled each other to pulp getting out of there. It wasn't until later, when they were sure the woman was really dead, that they returned and burned her body and her head on separate pyres.

The Indians were a superstitious lot, that much had been made clear during my brief acquaintance with them, but the wendigo incident was mystifying. Many years would pass before I understood that without any means of caring for the insane, the only logical asylum was death.

Meanwhile, life went on in the camp. Cameron, Stanley Simpson, the accountant, and I were trusted with shotguns and allowed to hunt. This meant we could provide food for the prisoners so that our captors wouldn't have to. We spent a lot of time roaming the countryside—the contract that kept us from escaping was the lives of the other prisoners—hunting fowl with great success. When the ice broke up off the creek, we speared dozens of jackfish that are always at their best when you're hungry.

By this time, Simpson had become a bit of a magician to the Indians. He had a glass eye that he removed for them, much to their amazement. Dressy Man was the most impressed because he himself was missing an eye. When he approached Simpson, he had replaced the breechclout and soot that he had worn to kill the wendigo with cloth pants and a swallow-tail coat that he had found at the fort during the ransacking. He was so enamoured of the black silk lining that he wore the coat inside out, then attached bells to the bottom that jingled wherever he went. He also wore a stovepipe hat, and considered himself at the top of the fashion world. He asked if Simpson's gods could provide him with a new eye. The accountant said he would see what he could do. He always carried a spare one with him and a couple of days later, he gave it to Dressy Man and showed him how to put it in. Dressy Man was thrilled, although he complained that he still could not see out of it. But he kept it in and was the first and last blue- and brown-eyed Indian I ever met.

The dancing and drumming in camp seemed to go on interminably, much of it attributable to a Dog Feast that was now in progress. The feast was a means of restoring the Indians' medicine to its full power, and they began by building a special lodge among the trees, using skins and willow branches. When it was finished, it looked more like a tunnel than a dwelling and I could easily see inside. Only the war chief and his councillors could sit in it and I stood outside with others, including Big Bear, and watched as they entered and took their places. As soon as they were seated, some women brought in a simmering kettle containing a cooked dog. Wandering Spirit, from his place of prominence, arose and danced around the kettle. He had a spear in his right hand and thrust it through the dog's head, amid war cries and applause from the others. Wandering Spirit then went to four of his bravest warriors—among them was Miserable Man—and led them, dancing, to a blanket spread out near the kettle. They sat down and ate from the pot, Wandering Spirit helping himself first. After he had finished, the others followed suit. The honoured warriors counted coup; Wandering Spirit topped them all with 15 slain, 13 of them Blackfoot and the last two Tom Quinn and Father Fafard. Once the coup counting was finished, the food was available for all to eat, including the prisoners. It didn't appeal to any of us and we made ourselves scarce so that we wouldn't have to refuse any offers. This was no time to be offending our captors.

Beyond the dances, the chiefs and councillors were constantly meeting, trying to decide on a course of action. Then a message arrived from Poundmaker, asking Big Bear and the Woods Cree to join him. He would have a gift of 60 cattle waiting, plus a hundred carts and horses. Together they would take Fort Battleford and the town, then go east to Batoche and join Riel in a great victory over all the whites. They would have their land back once more and the buffalo would return.

At the beginning of May, we were on the move again, only this time it was the entire camp. The grassy slopes of the hills were turning from their winter yellow to lush green, and all the trees were showing leaves. The weather was gloriously warm. Wandering Spirit led the way again while the other councillors rode up and down the long line of carts and dog- and pony-pulled travois, to keep everyone moving. At noon the entourage would stop for tea and to allow the animals to feed. Then we would march till evening, set up camp and listen to the infernal drums beating for half the night, and the speeches of personal derring-do. Wandering Spirit's echoed the loudest. "When we fought the Blackfoot we were afraid of nothing," he cried. "When the Queen's soldiers come I will lead the war cry of our people. If anyone fears to follow me they will die as the whites did at Frog Lake!"

And on it went. Some would fall asleep and others would awaken to take their place so that there was never an absence of noise in the camp. It was busy all the time and the only relief from it was short-lived slumber. One night a shot went off about 4:00 A.M., whether by accident or design we didn't know, but our first notion was that someone had tried to escape or they had begun killing the prisoners. Nothing came of it but it put us on edge even more.

We avoided Fort Pitt and went east another 10 miles, to Frenchman's Butte, a hill rather than a butte and once the site of an old trading post. While we travelled, several warriors rode to the ruins of the fort on the off chance that they had missed something during the ransacking. They returned with a few non-perishable items and some flour and bacon that had somehow escaped the holocaust. But this bonus was not without its consequences. One of the Plains Cree had stolen a Woods Cree's horse to make the journey to the fort and Wandering Spirit was furious about it. He recognized how strained the relations between the two bands already were and didn't want his warriors compounding the problem. Though it was a minor incident, it added to the growing resentment of the Plains people by their woodland counterparts, who had not fully supported rebelling in the first place. Instead, they viewed themselves as innocent bystanders, more or less swept up in events over which they had little control.

Now, some of the whites, McLean and Cameron in particular, were planting doubts in the woodland chiefs' minds, asking why they were listening to Big Bear's bidding, particularly when they outnumbered the Plains Cree three to one. Lucky Man and Cut Arm, chiefs from the Onion Lake Reserve, went to Big Bear and demanded his assurance that the rebellion was meeting with success. They didn't get it. Worse, just at that time, rumours came that Poundmaker had been defeated in a battle at Cut Knife Hill. But was it true? The Woods Cree were in a quandary.

The rumours of Poundmaker's defeat so depressed Big Bear that he resigned his leadership and Wandering Spirit, as war chief, became the de facto political leader. It was his contention that even if a battle had been lost, there was still a war to be won. Nevertheless, they needed more information. Had Poundmaker actually been defeated? And what was Riel's situation? The only sure way to find that out was to send scouts to Battleford or all the way to Batoche, if necessary. Since a journey that far would require several days, the scouts—Louis Goulet and an Indian—were dispatched posthaste. In the meantime, it was decided that a Thirst Dance would be held in order to heal the rift developing between the two bands.

The first thing needed was a lodge and to this end, several Indians went into the woods to find the poles for it. They selected a large, straight tree for the centre pole, actually hunted it and shot several bullets into it as if it were an enemy before chopping it down. They dragged it back to camp, whooping and firing their rifles in the air. The pole was set in a hole dug into the ground and they returned to the woods for the rafters, each one put in its special place around the centre pole and tied with rawhide where they intersected. They asked Cameron and me to participate in the placing of the poles, which we knew to be a great privilege. It was awkward at first, working side by side with my captors, but I soon found myself enjoying the camaraderie. And it was plain to see that this was serious business, to be done with great reverence. Once the framework was in place and hung with colourful decorations, the dancing began. All of the prisoners were invited to join in, but none of us did.

The following morning, the warriors filled a slight hollow with a huge pile of brush, and then disappeared. The old men, women and children stood by expectantly, as if some great game was about to begin. After everyone was settled, the warriors appeared from behind small rises and bushes and began to sneak up on the brush pile. It seemed to represent an enemy camp, and one of the warriors pretended to cut a hole in the side of a lodge, stab someone and then scalp him. All of the warriors then attacked the brush pile, taking away branches, as if they were horses, saying, "I have taken the *nasinasowatin* [pinto]," and "This *wanokawec* [chestnut] is mine." The women and children joined in and helped pull the pile apart, each carrying off a piece as a trophy, which they named. Then the warriors gave demonstrations of war tactics, from riding and shooting to digging rifle pits with their knives and firing at make-believe enemies. I thought at first I was a witnessing a literal "theatre of war" but it occurred to me later that it might very well have been a rehearsal.

There was more dancing that night and I half looked forward to the next day when the event would culminate with the braves skewering themselves and dancing around the pole until they were in enough of a trance to withstand the pain of tearing themselves away. But we never got to see it.

Louis Goulet and his fellow scout returned early the following morning, before the ceremony began. They had got nearly as far as Battleford when several people informed them that Poundmaker had indeed suffered a defeat. Even more alarming, many "policemen"—a term the Indians commonly used for soldiers—were on their way from Edmonton and Battleford with a single purpose: they were going "Bear hunting."

The Indians had barely digested this unwelcome bit of news when a lookout rode into camp at a gallop. Through field glasses stolen from Fort Pitt, he had spotted the white tents and blue uniforms of the "hunters," just a few miles to the west.

TWELVE

Frenchman's Butte

THERE WAS NEAR PANDEMONIUM in the camp. Wearing only a breechclout, moccasins and two bandoliers crisscrossed over his chest, Wandering Spirit vaulted onto the grey mare and rode among the lodges, shouting war cries and brandishing his Winchester. Little Poplar was dressed similarly, but in addition he wore a beaver-felt top hat adorned with a single feather and a snugly fitting waistcoat that made him look like a half-dressed drum major preparing to lead a parade. His face was painted red and yellow, and he waved his rifle in the air and sang a war song. When he finished, he called out his contempt for the Woods Cree who were not responding to the emergency the way he wanted them to.

"Are the Woods Cree going to sit in their lodges like women, quivering at the sight of a few Red Coats, waiting to be knocked on the head like rabbits?"

His biting words shamed them into action and they stripped down and painted their bodies to prepare for battle. Several warriors formed a patrol and went to fend off the soldiers while the rest of us hurriedly decamped and moved out to find a more defendable position.

Two miles to the northeast, we followed the swampy valley of a tributary of the Little Red Deer River. To our right was a high, poplar-covered ridge, to our left a bluff with its slope and front edge barren of trees. Farther along the valley, a ravine cut off to the left. We turned up it, picking our way through the trees to the far end, which allowed access to the bluff and a view of the valley and the ridge opposite. The Indians decided to make a stand there.

They dug rifle pits in the side of the ravine and along the top of the bluff, and disguised the mounds of earth removed from the pits by planting tree branches in them. Then they strung a bolt of red calico in the trees to bait the trap, theorizing that the soldiers would be compelled to investigate it.

They made us dig several refuge pits nearby for ourselves. These were four to five feet deep; some of the prisoners piled bags of flour around the edges for added protection, while others used felled trees. I noticed that Amelia and Eliza helped their father chop down the trees for their pit, the only women to do so. Once the work was completed, we could only wait to see if the soldiers came up the valley and into the Indians' gunsights, though none of us figured they would be foolish enough to follow the obvious trail we had left without reconnoitring first. To any military mind, it was a perfect place for an ambush.

I shared a pit with Cameron, Reverend Charles Quinney and his wife, and three half-breeds from Onion Lake that I didn't know. We were all nervous but Mrs. Quinney was terrified and on the verge of tears. Her husband kept reassuring her that we would soon be rescued.

Wandering Spirit came and squatted at the edge of our pit. War paint streaked his face and body and madness streaked his dark eyes. As usual, he carried his rifle, as much a part of him now as his other appendages. Pointing it at us, he swung it in a broad arc so that each of us came under its gaping muzzle, a term I use advisedly because it is astonishing how large that normally small hole can seem when it's aimed directly at your heart.

"You must not try to warn the police of our position. I will kill you if you do," he said. He swung the rifle in a reverse arc and was gone.

No one truly believed that we would need to warn anybody. As far as we were concerned our rescue was imminent, if the Indians didn't kill us first. They would not be able to match the fire power of the soldiers, and any battle begun would be a battle short-lived.

That night the patrol returned, riding in breathlessly with the news that the soldiers' advance was swift and they would soon be upon us. A warrior named Meeminook had been lost in a brief skirmish with them. This was sad news for Cameron who considered Meeminook a good friend. During the spring of 1884, when Cameron was heading toward the Onion Lake area with some trade items, Meeminook had guided him over part of the trail. They spoke only Cree on the journey and it improved Cameron's grasp of the language immensely. After the massacre, when he was still under threat by Wandering Spirit, Meeminook showed up and told him not to worry.

"While I am in camp, Wandering Spirit will need to be careful how he even looks at you, especially if he loves his life," he had said.

Cameron believed he owed Meeminook a huge debt and had now lost the opportunity to repay it.

A long night passed into a morning grey with fog. Crystal droplets of dew hung from the trees and grass. Except for bird calls, all was silent in the valley and along the bluff. The Indians were nervous. They didn't like the fog and what it could hide. When the sun rose and burned away the cloak of concealment, a lookout spotted a soldier among the poplars on the ridge opposite the bluff. Almost simultaneously a cannon boomed, and an explosive thud followed by the sound of cascading branches came from somewhere behind us. I noticed that Cameron's eyes were as wide as mine. "That one was long," he said. "When they find the right range, we're going to be in serious trouble!"

I didn't say anything but I was worried. After we had survived for so long it would be a terrible irony to be done in by our rescuers. Other shots followed, still well over our heads, interspersed with rifle fire from the Indians. The battle had begun in earnest. An old woman, frightened by the pounding of the big gun, lamented, "Spare our children today, oh Sun, and I will give to you a looking glass!" This we interpreted as meaning that the sun, as vain as a beautiful woman, would love to gaze upon its own face.

Wandering Spirit ran up and down behind the rifle pits shouting words of encouragement to his warriors. One suffered a bullet wound to his wrist and staggered back from the bluff, bleeding profusely. The Woods Cree, as well as some of the older Plains Cree concerned for our safety, decided to move us beyond the range of the cannon. They led us away in groups: the first included Amelia and her family, the second Mary Gowanlock, Theresa Delaney, John Pritchard, his wife and their children, and finally our small band— Cameron, the Quinneys, the half-breeds and me. We were taken to a different area than the other groups and knew it might be deliberate. The question, though, was why? My hunch was that if we had to go on the run, the soldiers would be faced with the dilemma of choosing which trail to follow.

We could hear the battle continuing sporadically throughout most of the morning. The Indians complained bitterly of the unfairness of the powerful cannon, which they called the "gun that speaks twice," referring to the noise of the weapon firing and the shell exploding into shrapnel when it hit. These had become muffled sounds off in the distance and were now music to our ears. Then reports came back to us that the soldiers had lost many men and were in retreat.

We could scarcely believe it; didn't want to believe it, in fact, because it brought our soaring spirits plummeting earthward. The only thing that kept them from crashing completely was a kernel of good news: during the battle, Man Who Speaks Another Tongue had been hit in the stomach with shrapnel and severely injured. Those of us from Frog Lake had to suppress a resounding cheer.

In the afternoon, Chief Cut Arm joined our small group. He wore a coat blanket pulled in at the waist with a belt, and a fox-skin cap. Attached to the belt was a sheathed knife, the only weapon he ever carried. He'd had his left arm amputated after receiving a bullet wound from a Blackfoot, and could not use a rifle. He ordered us to move again. We were heading north and Quinney, who considered himself Cut Arm's friend, asked why we weren't pursuing the soldiers if the Indians had defeated them. The chief said that the warriors were so low on ammunition that pursuit was impractical. The plan was to swing northeast to Loon Lake to gather resources in order to continue the fight. Big Bear and Wandering Spirit were flanking us to the west with the other prisoners in tow.

Our captors had not allowed us to bring our tents so we had only personal items and blankets in our possession as we moved slowly north of the battle site. The woods were thick and broken up mainly by marshes. Cut Arm had us spread out as much as possible to make the trail we left less easy to follow. It was a futile ploy and I broke branches whenever I could do it without being detected; any tracker worth his salt could have followed them.

We camped that night in a despondent mood and none of the captives, including me, had much to say. We had believed we were on the brink of rescue and now it seemed as far away as the prairie moon that pierced the foliage with shafts of light. We huddled in our blankets as a dank fog descended again and brought with it a profound silence. We slept in fits and starts and awoke in the morning cold and damp, in an even darker frame of mind, with rain seeping through the trees.

Later, we heard an occasional gunshot far to the west of us, but it didn't sound like battle fire. Cameron thought it was shotguns, most likely Big Bear's group hunting rabbits for food. The rest of that day and the next we moved northeast, through rolling parkland of open prairie interspersed with stands of poplar. But the farther north we moved, the more forested the terrain became, much of it dense spruce that slowed our pace drastically. A cold rain continued and we were chilled to our marrow crossing a swollen stream. There was a strong current running and it would have been easy just to drift away on it but the possible consequences were unthinkable.

There was never enough food. We ate wild carrots and killed ducklings we found at the edges of the many ponds we passed, and supplemented this sparse fare with bannock but only at night when we stopped to build a fire. The Indians were hungry too and we used that as fodder to chisel away at Cut Arm's resolve to keep us prisoners. Quinney did most of the talking, working also on the feelings of guilt that he knew the chief harboured.

"Seekaskootch, [Cut Arm]," he said, "I owe you my life. Your kindness, when you escorted me to Fort Pitt, saved me from the same fate as my white brothers at Frog Lake. Did you do that only to have my life placed in jeopardy once again?"

Cut Arm replied, "You are safe as long as you are with me."

"That may be so. But you have no guarantees that it will remain so. When we join up with Big Bear again, what will he do? Maybe he has already killed the other prisoners and has the same plans for us at Loon Lake."

"I would not let him kill you."

"But you might not have any say in the matter. Besides, what will you do with us? Continue to feed us when you can scarcely feed your own people?"

At every opportunity, Quinney worked on Cut Arm and in time, the minister finally got him to admit openly that he did not want to be here anymore than we did. Nevertheless, he was still reluctant to let us go. "If I set you free and Big Bear finds you, he will kill you," Cut Arm said. "Then I would be as responsible for your deaths as he. If he did not find you, then he might want to kill me and I do not wish to fight Big Bear."

Quinney and Cut Arm spoke as if it were Big Bear we ought to be afraid of but I didn't believe that for a moment. I think what they were really talking about were the warriors such as Wandering Spirit, Miserable Man, Little Poplar and Little Bad Man. They were the ones we needed to fear most while the Cree remained in a state of war.

The last day of May was a Sunday, miserable and wet; nevertheless Quinney held a service among the trees for those who felt a need for it, which included pretty well all of us. We never knew from one day to the next if we would find freedom or death, only that it had to be one or the other, and the strain of living with that knowledge over such a long period was taking its toll on everyone. Most days we recognized that we needed to stay united, but tempers ran short and we occasionally caught ourselves snapping at each other.

Once, while crossing a log, I momentarily lost my balance and grabbed Cameron's arm. It was near the end of another long day, we were exhausted, and I nearly pulled both of us to the ground. He shook my hand off and complained. "Watch where you're going, Jack, I can't carry you!" His reaction startled me and so did mine. I was angry and wanted to lash out at him. But he apologized. "I'm sorry," he said. "I didn't mean that."

"I know, Bill," I said. "Don't worry about it."

I did not tell him that I had felt like hitting him.

Reverend Quinney was sensitive to everyone's mental condition, and that evening spoke briefly of the pressures on us and prayed for God's guidance. It was a simple prayer, in plain language, that ended in a plea for our freedom and our lives, and though I had never found much succour in religious services, to that I could say "Amen." He had Cameron interpret the prayer in Cree for the benefit of our captors who were watching with considerable interest.

The following morning, Cut Arm and his councillors held a meeting. They kept us far enough away that we couldn't hear their actual words; nevertheless, the discussion sounded heated and went on for some time. Then Cut Arm rose from the circle in which they had gathered and walked over to where we sat. It was plain by his demeanour that he carried the weight of a momentous decision on his shoulders.

Addressing Reverend Quinney he said, "I have always been your friend. When they told me of the killings at Frog Lake, I went to Big Bear and told him that I was very sorry about what happened. Wandering Spirit threatened to kill me and I told him that I was not afraid of him, even though I have only one good arm. I told him it was a shame that he had

murdered innocent white people and I did not want him
doing the same to you. That is what I said. That is why I took
you to Fort Pitt. For many years, my people have lived in
friendship with the Company and with the people of your
churches. Your hearts have always been in the right place,
though I cannot say the same for your heads. We do not have
a fight with you. It is with your government. We cannot blame
you for what they decide any more than I can blame my people
for what I decide. We have kept you from your homes for too
long and now you must return. We will not stop you."

"And what of our friends with Big Bear?" asked Quinney. "If
they are still alive, will they not be killed because we are free?"

"I will speak for them. I will see that no harm comes to
them. You have my word."

"And what about you, my friend? What about you and Big
Bear?"

"I will deal with him when the time comes."

"And Wandering Spirit and Miserable Man? Can you
deal with them, too?"

I was impatient for Quinney to accept Cut Arm's decision
without all the fuss. I recognized his concern for the others
and for his friend, and that there was more involved than just
our freedom, but I wanted us to be on our way. I'd had enough
of the sheer monotony and discomfort of traipsing across the
countryside and expecting danger every waking hour.

The chief said, "We have not been honest with you. We
spoke with two tongues because we had to. We did not defeat
the police. They retreated for the same reason we did—they
ran out of ammunition. They will return with their big guns

and will try to destroy us. Wandering Spirit and Miserable Man will need us as allies, but that will only come to pass if they release your friends."

"You give much, my friend," said Quinney, and there was a catch in his throat.

We each shook Cut Arm's hand in turn, thanked him, and were gone from the camp in the time it took to gather our meagre possessions. We kept looking back along our trail to see if anyone was following us but we were alone. After six weeks of captivity for me, and two months for Cameron, we were free at last.

We had come about 70 miles from Frog Lake and about 35 from Fort Pitt, 25 of those from Frenchman's Butte, and reckoned that we wouldn't have to retrace our tracks much farther than that to find the soldiers. Invigorated by our freedom, the seven of us set out at a pace we could not have matched had we still been with Cut Arm. By following the trail we had made we had no need for any bushwhacking, so we put the miles swiftly behind us. We passed through the same woods, crossed the same small prairies and streams, and skirted the same ponds and marshes as we had on our trip north, but there was a new light on everything and it was like travelling through a new country. Even recrossing the large stream was no hardship. The sombre mood that had marked our passage had disappeared with our new-found freedom. After a scant supper of wild carrots, we reached the battle site and descended through the ravine, past the rifle pits and into the valley. By then we were exhausted, especially Mrs. Quinney who could barely walk.

We were preparing a camp for the night when we heard a noise so familiar I nearly cried out in joy: a steamboat whistle, carried from the river on the evening breeze. The sound evoked cries of delight and revived us but after a brief discussion it was agreed that only Cameron and I would make first contact with the soldiers. The others would stay behind with Mrs. Quinney so that she could rest and if all went well, we would have someone return with a horse for her.

After a brief respite, Cameron and I struck out down the valley, our feet sore but our spirits in fine form. The weather had cleared over the course of the day and stars were showing themselves faintly in the eastern sky. Where it wasn't swampy, the valley floor was badly churned up but not at all difficult for two men on foot. We were nearing the site of the Thirst Dance lodge when we heard the sound of thudding hooves.

We presumed it was soldiers but were skittish enough to think that it might be Indians. Just in case, we took cover behind some willow bushes and watched as two riders approached. In the dusky light, we couldn't tell at first if they were friend or foe but when we recognized the military uniforms we could not contain ourselves and leaped from our hiding place. Startled, the horses reared and the soldiers drew their pistols.

"Don't shoot!" we yelled in unison. "Don't shoot!"

Then Cameron said, "I'm Bill Cameron and this is Jack Strong. From Frog Lake!"

I don't know what those soldiers thought of the two of us, standing there in our ragged, filthy clothes and worn moccasins but we had a mighty high opinion of them. They were with the Alberta Field Force and were bivouacked in a meadow a mile or so from where we had left our friends. They had just come from the steamboat that had brought supplies up from Fort Battleford and were returning to their camp.

The soldiers dismounted and let Cameron and me enjoy the luxury of riding back to our companions. We rained questions upon the soldiers and discovered that the rebellion was all but over. General Middleton and his forces had crushed Riel and his rebels at Batoche. All that was left now was to tie up a few loose ends, one of them being the capture of Big Bear and those responsible for the murders at Frog Lake and Fort Pitt.

We couldn't see the faces of our friends as we helloed them in the fast-dying light, but didn't need to. Mrs. Quinney's sobs of relief and joy spoke for everyone. Quinney himself was crying, clutching one of the soldier's arms in gratitude and disbelief. Cameron and I gave up the horses to the minister and his wife.

At the soldiers' camp, we were taken immediately to the commanding officer's tent for debriefing. Major General T. Bland Strange, commander of the Alberta Field Force, lay stretched out on his cot as we entered but sprang quickly to his feet. A retired British officer known to his friends as "Jingo," his prominent chest and strutting manner reminded me of Dickens, only more so. He was balding but made up for the lack of hair on his head with a black, bushy beard that hid his lower face and neck. His gaze was as direct as his questions.

While we provided answers, an aide brought both Cameron and me some bacon and beans and rum, a cup each, filled to the top. I took a huge swallow and nearly choked on it but revelled in the pleasurable feeling that flooded my weary, overtaxed body. We told the general everything we knew, right up to where we left Cut Arm and his warriors and how they were going to meet Big Bear at Loon Lake.

Strange then told us about the battle north of Frenchman's Butte that we, as prisoners, had only listened to. When the soldiers arrived at the valley's edge, opposite the bluff on which the Indians and we were entrenched, they had seen the red bolt of calico in the trees and correctly surmised it was bait for a trap. Through field glasses, Strange saw the freshly dug rifle pits and fake trees. After a brief discussion with his officers, he decided to try to outflank the Indians, but it ultimately proved impossible. Their left side was too well defended, and the valley floor leading to the right was too swampy. He set up his cannon on the ridge and hoped its fire would pin the Indians down while his troops descended into the broad valley. That was as far as they got. The terrain was too soft and the horses sank to their chests. Even had they been able to cross the morass, the slope up to the Indians' position was too steep and bare, providing no cover whatsoever. Strange's men fired up the hill at anything that moved and, between cannon shots, the Indians showered the soldiers with rifle fire. Luckily, this consisted largely of musket balls and shotgun pellets that fell short of their target or lacked the power to cause serious injury.

After three hours of exchanging fire, the soldiers ran low on ammunition and retreated to the ridge; a few men were bruised from musket balls and one was wounded. Strange then decided to fall even farther back and wait for Middleton, who was coming to provide assistance. Strange didn't find out until some time later that the Indians had also retreated. When the soldiers investigated the battle site, they found many of the items stolen by the Indians at Frog Lake, Onion Lake and Fort Pitt. There was a king's ransom in furs, along with bacon, flour and other items ranging from tools to silverware. Only then did they know that they had won the battle and that the enemy had fled in a panic.

I slept on a cot that night for the first time in weeks and, between the exhaustion from the long day's trek and the cup of rum I couldn't finish, nothing short of booming cannons could have awakened me. In the morning, after donning a fresh change of clothing and used boots scrounged from the civilian teamsters, I breakfasted with Cameron and our fellow ex-prisoners, and everyone was chatty and happy. We had celebrity status among the soldiers who treated us with no small degree of respect tinged with awe. Afterward, General Strange summoned Cameron and me to his tent. He was with a North-West Mounted Police major.

"Gentlemen," Strange said. "This is Major Steele, commanding officer of the North-West Mounted Police and a Scout contingent. There is something we would ask of you."

Steele was a burly man who held himself ramrod straight and seemed as sturdy as his name implied. He had a neatly trimmed, inverted V-shaped moustache and shaved the hair around his ears close to his head. He looked more of a military man than Strange. He asked for our names and smiled at mine.

"Would that be Wild Jack?" he asked.

I'm not sure he'd ever read a Wild Jack Strong book but I'd wager that some of his men had and I doubted anything that they did, right down to the smallest detail, ever escaped his attention.

I grinned back. "Not yet, sir."

He shook our hands warmly and said how pleased he was with our release. "I expect your experience was unpleasant indeed," he added. "It might have killed lesser men. But right now we have some women to worry about."

He mentioned Theresa Gowanlock, Mary Delaney and the McLean girls, and that newspapers were already reporting that they were being "outraged" by the Indians.

Spreading a map out on a table, Strange spoke next. "Gentlemen, we have Riel and now we want Big Bear. The hand we will nab him with is four fingered. By that I mean four columns of troops will make their way north from various points along the river to trap him." Pointing a bony finger at the map he said, "One column will leave Prince Albert and move northwest to cut off our quarry should he turn east from Loon Lake. Another column will leave from Fort Battleford to prevent an escape to the southeast. General Middleton, when he arrives, will go north from here, and I will go to Frog Lake and strike north from there, just in case the Bear flees to the west. Meanwhile, Major Steele and his Scouts will hasten north until General Middleton and his troops can relieve them."

He paused and took a sip of water from a cup on the table. "Mr. Cameron, you are fluent in Cree and you, Mr. Strong, by your own account, know enough of the language to get by. And just as important, not only do you know Big Bear but you can identify the trouble makers as well, particularly the murderers from Frog Lake. Since Big Bear knows and trusts you, there's also a small chance that you could talk him into surrendering before there's bloodshed. On the other hand, if a battle should ensue, the Cree shout orders and directions just as we do, and it is to our advantage to have men who can understand them. So what we would ask of you is this: Will one of you ride with me and the other with Major Steele in our efforts to bring the Bear and his henchmen to justice? I will not discount the risks involved. You know what they are as well as I do. The decision is yours to make, gentlemen. I would add that after what you've been through, no one would think less of you should you decline."

I didn't have to think about my answer. Nor did Cameron. I could guess why he wanted to go but I *knew* why I did: the women, especially Amelia. I wanted to see them all returned to safety, and I wanted the Frog Lake murderers brought to justice.

"I'm ready to go, sir, whenever you are," I said, and Cameron seconded my sentiments.

Since I was already a duly sworn-in Special Constable with the NWMP, I rode with Steele, who supplied me with a blanket, rifle, revolver, two belts of ammunition and a horse. My pay would be "Two dollars a day," he said, clearly proud of the government's generosity. As Steele's men had been responsible for providing their own horses and equipment and I had neither, he kindly waived those costs, citing special circumstances. However, if I happened to lose anything due to carelessness, especially the horse, the government's generous position would be re-examined.

I scarcely slept that night. I don't know why but every single person I knew or had known, alive or now dead, passed through my mind in a long procession of reacquaintance. I dallied with Amelia and wondered how she was. Would her intelligence and confidence see her through? I didn't know and I was afraid for her. Somewhere among those ramblings, I must have fallen asleep, for Steele's shouting rudely awakened me, "Get up, men! Grab eight days' half-rations and follow me!"

That was at 2:00 A.M. Within the hour, 68 mounted men and 75 horses were on the trail of Big Bear.

THIRTEEN

The Chase

WE RODE OUT IN TWO COLUMNS composed of North-West Mounted Police officers, Alberta Mounted Rifles and Steele's volunteer Scouts, but all wore buckskins and Stetsons, except the major, who wore his scarlet tunic and white helmet, and me, in borrowed civilian clothes. We also wore bandoliers, heavy with ammunition, and rifles lay horizontally across our saddles, kept there by special holders attached to the horn.

I rode alongside Steele because of my familiarity with the area, and I would be less than truthful if I didn't admit to a modicum of pride. As an officer and as a man, he was everything that Dickens wasn't. He inspired confidence in all that he did, from the way he carried himself to the way he spoke. He sat a horse as if he were part of the animal. In a time when men, too often of prominence rather than substance, bought themselves officer's commissions, Steele had earned his by working his way through the ranks. Now an NWMP inspector, he acquired the militia equivalent of major when General Strange asked him to form a scouting unit to spearhead the Alberta Field Force. He was a tough commander who always expected the best from his men and gave the same in return, never asking them to do anything that he wouldn't do himself. And he was completely unflappable, not from a lack of understanding about what was going on around him but from an intelligent assessment of it.

Beyond the camp, we came across several tracks branching out like the spines of a fan. Steele had inspected these the day before.

"Which do you suppose is Big Bear's?" he asked, more to test my knowledge than because he needed an answer.

I didn't know, but I knew which one was Cut Arm's because it was as familiar as a twice-read novel.

"I can't say, sir," I said. "But I don't think it matters. As I said at the debriefing, Cut Arm told us they were all going to gather at Loon Lake. These tracks are just meant to confuse us and slow us down. They'll all join up sooner or later."

"What if he was lying to you? What if he was the decoy?"

"I don't think he was lying, sir. He seemed more like a man at the end of his rope to me, with no reason to lie."

"Well, let's go see if you're right," he said and spurred his magnificent black forward.

We followed the widest track but Steele wasn't a man to take chances. He sent Scouts along the others to see if any of them diverged widely from the general direction of Loon

Lake. None did, and in fact a couple of them even merged, at which point we found a fresh burial mound.

"Let's find out what's underneath," Steele said. "I can't imagine that the Indians would waste time burying a prisoner but we'll make sure." He ordered two of his men to open the grave.

I stood aside and watched as they began to dig. The grave was shallow and even though I had not heard it before, I recognized the sound of metal thumping against flesh and bone. They reached the body in short order and when it was only partly exposed, it was evident that it was an Indian. Using his hand, one of the Scouts brushed the dirt away from the corpse's face.

"Do you recognize him, Strong?" asked Steele.

You bet I recognized him and he didn't look any less belligerent in death than he had in life. "Yes, sir," I said. "It's Kahweechetwaymot, Man Who Speaks Another Tongue. He's one of the murderers from Frog Lake."

"Capital," said Steele. "It will save the expense of a trial and hanging him."

But not only was he a murderer, he was also the man whose actions I had read about in the newspaper at Joe's place, which had brought me here in the first place. I could not have conjured this scene in a thousand years.

The Scouts filled in the grave more quickly than they had opened it and it was not a scene on which to dwell. A strange satisfaction sifted through me. It may be that a man should not feel satisfied to see another man dead but I could not help myself. And disgusting though his unearthed corpse was, the sight would never replace that of seeing him shoot Father Fafard in the face.

Under way again, we'd travelled only a few hundred yards when we heard shouting, in English, and saw a skeleton of a man in tattered clothing coming down the trail toward us. It was John Pritchard, his face a mixture of astonishment and profound gratitude. My heart flew into my mouth and I feared the worst for the lives of Theresa Delaney and Mary Gowanlock, because Pritchard had been their protector and now he was alone. My fears, however, were unfounded. He was camped just up the trail with his family and the two women, had heard our approach and come to greet us. They had all been with Big Bear and when his warriors spotted us, the band had fled so quickly that they ignored the prisoners, presuming that Pritchard, since he was part Indian, would follow along. He didn't. Instead, he took the opportunity to escape. He loaded his family and the women on his wagon and retreated as fast as he could drive, forging a trail over creeks and logs so rough that Mary had been thrown out and hurt her back.

Pritchard led us to their camp, a single tent and a wagon that appeared ready to fall apart. As we rode up, Mrs. Pritchard, holding a toddler in one arm, was making bannock over a small fire with her older children gathered around. Mary hobbled out of the tent, the image of some poor street urchin destined for the orphanage, and upon seeing us sat down painfully and wept. Behind her came Theresa whose eyes flew wide in astonishment at the sight of me, the only familiar face among her rescuers. She tried to smile but it was more like a grimace. She looked terrible. Her robustness had given way to frailty and her fair skin was raw from exposure to the sun and wind. Her lips were so cracked and dry it was little wonder she couldn't smile. Like Mary's, her clothes were rags and her hair was unkempt. I jumped down from my horse and in three strides had her in my arms. She let the tears go then, and I could feel her body quivering against mine.

"Jack! Oh, Jack!" she cried. "Oh, Lord, it's wonderful to see you! How ever did you manage to get away?"

The question required too long an answer, so I said only, "You're safe now, Theresa. It's over."

No one was happier about that fact than I. A part of me still insisted that I had deserted her and Mary when I ran like a scared rabbit from Frog Lake and left their fate in the hands of the Indians. I wanted their forgiveness but it was neither the time nor the place to ask for it.

I hugged Mary, too. She was skin and bone, her sweet oval face now angular and smudged with tears. I squeezed her lightly but it still caused her to groan from her sore back. When I apologized, she managed a smile and said, "It was worth it, Jack. Never has a little bit of pain felt so good."

She asked about Cameron and was visibly relieved to hear that he was well enough to be in on the hunt for Big Bear. Then there was a strange silence among those gathered round her. An unspoken question hung in the air. "No," Mary said, knowing instinctively what it was. "We were not outraged by the Indians. This is not to say that we weren't afraid of the possibility almost every waking hour. I don't know how many times we looked at the tent door only to see a wicked eye staring back us. But they did not lay a hand on us, praise God, and Mr. Pritchard, for without him we would not have been so fortunate."

There was another moment of awkward silence, as if Mary's words were too intimate for ordinary men to hear. Then Steele changed tack and asked, "Were the McLeans with you?"

Theresa answered. "Yes, but we hardly ever saw them because they were separated from us. Big Bear always kept Mr. McLean close to him, so they were usually in a different part of the camp."

That Big Bear would want to keep close tabs on McLean made a lot of sense and indicated why Amelia and her family were still captives and not dead. The Bear would be a fool to let them go or kill them, as McLean would be an ideal negotiator as well as a bargaining chip.

I thanked John Pritchard for saving my friends' lives. He could scarcely speak, he was so emotional. He had taken complete responsibility for the women during the two months of their captivity and hardly saw a day when he wasn't faced, at some point, with the possibility of having to give his life for theirs. That he might leave his children fatherless only increased the stress on him. Now that their ordeal had finally ended, he was weak with relief.

Steele ordered some canned beef and biscuits for the rescued party and had their minor cuts and contusions attended to. He then assigned two men to escort them back to the safety of the Alberta Field Force camp.

We set out again and I was lighter of heart, with yet another hurdle behind me. Within a few miles we entered a narrow valley where all of the trails we had been scouting converged into one.

"Top marks for you, Strong," Steele said, complimenting me for my prediction that this would eventually happen. It added an inch or so to my height and was yet another of Steele's strengths as commander, that he would give praise when praise was due. For the most part I wasn't telling him anything he didn't already know or hadn't at least guessed, but he appreciated that I possessed knowledge enough to confirm it.

The Indians had abandoned more of their loot in the valley: carts, furs, even some food. There were dozens of cold campfires, which indicated that several hundred of them had set up lodges. On the hillsides there were more rifle pits. It was a place of ambush that they had decided, for some reason, not to use.

We found a note that lifted my spirits and eased the hard lines on Steele's face a little. It was a scrap of paper affixed to a piece of red cloth attached to a twig and contained a message from McLean himself. It read, "We have moved northeast from here. We are all well. May God protect us. W.J. McLean. May 27, 1885."

Five days had passed since they were here. We didn't need the note to tell us which direction they had moved, as the trail was obvious, but it did confirm our belief that the McLean family and the other hostages were still alive.

Beyond the valley, the terrain became incredibly difficult as we struggled through thick spruce forests and across spongy marshes. The Indians had done their best to thwart any would-be trackers by toppling trees across the trail. Some, still partly attached to their trunks, were difficult to remove, because in our haste to leave camp, we had not brought a single axe.

The Indians had also laid traps for us by digging holes in the ground large enough to trip an animal and break its leg, disguising them with a thin covering of twigs and leaves. This forced us to move more slowly than we wanted but even then, a few horses had to be put down because of broken legs or torn ligaments. Their riders had to return to camp, carrying their saddles over their shoulders. None of them had come this far to turn back and did not leave without grumbling about it.

Any open areas now were invariably swampy and hard for the horses to traverse. As the sun rose, the deer flies and mosquitoes attacked us in full force. The men cursed. The mud from the muskeg was all that kept the animals from being driven into a frenzy. In a small, dry meadow, Steele ordered a halt for lunch and asked for two Scouts to check out the trail ahead.

"I'll go, sir," I said, eager to be the first to catch a glimpse of our quarry, although I'm certain Steele would have asked me anyway in the likelihood that I might recognize anyone we spotted.

Jim "Jumbo" Fisk, a tall, dishevelled Calgarian in his early 20s, was the other volunteer. He had joined Steele's Scouts in hopes of killing a "fuckin' Indian or two," and opportunity was knocking. Had I been able to choose, I would have picked someone else to ride with me. Not only did Jumbo have blinders on when it came to the Indians, he also lived up to his nickname. He was clumsy and seemed to me to be a disaster in the making.

"Have a quick bite to eat," Steele said. "Then off you go. Move slow and keep your heads up. My guess is that we're not far behind them."

Jumbo was anxious to get moving as we washed down a biscuit and a bit of canned beef with some water, and so was I but for different reasons. I wasn't interested in killing anybody; I just wanted to see the hostages rescued and the murderers from Frog Lake brought to justice. We climbed on our horses and urged them across the meadow to where the trail re-entered the forest.

Jumbo led and we moved as slowly and quietly as possible, our eyes scanning ahead for any sign of traps, movement or anything that didn't fit in. We skirted a trip-hole that was so obvious it might have been made that way on purpose to lure us into something more deadly, but there was nothing else. And except for the odd, far-off bird call and the plodding horses the woods were as silent as a graveyard. Too silent for my liking. I levered a bullet into the chamber of my rifle and held it in my hand, the barrel pointing skyward and the butt of the stock resting on my thigh. Jumbo rode with one hand on his revolver. Every minute or so we stopped and listened.

Then, amid the bird sounds, we heard a sudden rustle of leaves. I caught some movement out of the corner of my eye and Jumbo did too, but before either of us could react, two quick rifle shots broke the silence. Jumbo yelped in pain as a bullet tore off a finger on his left hand and shattered his elbow. As he turned his horse and flew past me, hell-bent toward the meadow, I saw two Indians on horseback galloping off down the trail.

Without thinking, I spurred my horse and went after them, riding faster than I ought to over that treacherous ground. I didn't care about whether or not I was being drawn into a trap. The ambushers disappeared beyond a low rise before I could squeeze off a shot and I dismounted, ran to the crest and threw myself to the ground, crawling to where I could peer over. They were nowhere in sight. I listened for the horse hooves but all I could hear was my heart pounding in my ears. I lay checking everything in my field of vision for movement. I saw nothing. It was only then that I realized what I'd done and that I was trembling. I was returning to my horse just as Steele arrived at a gallop.

"We saw them, sir!" I said excitedly. "They're gone!"

"I take it you've no bullet holes in need of attention, Strong," he said.

"No, sir. I'm fine. But I never even got a shot off!"

"You'll get your chance," he said. "Now hustle back and bring the men here as quickly as possible. The faster we get after them, the less time they'll have to prepare for us."

He swung off his horse and, taking field glasses from his saddlebag, went forward to the rise while I went back for the rest of the men. I was glad he hadn't seen me go flying off after the Indians the way I had because I don't think he would have approved. Had it actually been a trap I'd have been a lot worse off than Jumbo Fisk. Yet it felt much better to be chasing the Indians than having them chase me.

Jumbo was bandaged and sent back to camp, angry that his personal mission had gone unfulfilled.

We pressed hard now, moving as swiftly as the terrain would allow. Late in the afternoon we stopped briefly for a half ration of biscuits, then carried on, through twilight and into the night. If there were any complaints, the men kept them to themselves. The trail continued to be rugged and even more men had to retreat because of horses either worn out or injured. We halted for another bite to eat just before dawn while another advance patrol went ahead. They were back in 20 minutes. Loon Lake and the Indians were just over the next ridge.

"Come with me, Strong," Steele ordered. To an NCO he said, "Bring up the rest of the men when they've finished eating."

I quickly gulped down what was left of my morning ration and mounted. We rode forward with the patrol sergeant-major, a likeable Irishman named Bill Fury, through an open, bushy area interspersed with poplars. At the ridge we dismounted near a huge, flat boulder. Dawn was just breaking and to the northeast, we could clearly see the lake.

The gentle slope below us was treed, the underbrush trampled by the Indians' passage. At the bottom was a small creek and beyond that a meadow, enclosed on the left by low hills and on the right by a spruce-and-tamarack swamp edging the lake. In the meadow, a couple of wagons stood beside three lodges, and a handful of Indians were going about the business of decamping, looking unconcerned. Farther on, past the camp and more trees, some other Indians were fording a narrow neck of water that ran north and south. On the east side of the neck, the land rose steeply on what Steele guessed was a peninsula since we could see plenty of water beyond the narrows. He speculated that the water below and to the right of us was a bay of the main lake.

"I think they're abandoning their camp, sir," said Fury.

"Maybe," said Steele. "But it could be a trap, too. They could be waiting for us to descend from this ridge, and we'd be sitting ducks once we reached the clearing." He asked, "Recognize anybody down there, Strong?"

While I couldn't make out any facial features from that distance, I didn't need to. I recognized the hair and the regalia. "Yes, sir," I said. "The one with the long, curly hair over by the lodges is Wandering Spirit."

"Just the man we're looking for," said Steele and in a split-second made his decision. "Right. If we want to save the prisoners we'll have to go down there, and go down fast."

We waited only a short while before the rest of the men rode up and dismounted. Steele climbed onto the flat boulder and had them count off in consecutive numbers and remember whether they were odd or even. "We're going down, men." he said. "We'll split into two columns at the bottom. Odd numbers follow Sergeant-Major Fury. Your job will be to climb the hill on the left and clear it of any Indians who might be waiting in ambush. The rest of you follow me. We'll take the camp. Check your weapons." He turned to me. "You stay with me, Strong, and tell me if you hear anything I should know about."

Steele removed his revolver from its holster and checked it, and once everyone was ready we moved off on foot down the slope. We were nearly 50 strong and descended boldly, without concern for noise. I had never known such excitement in all my life and rather than think about what might be waiting for us at the bottom, I concentrated on trying not to trip. Yet I was attuned to everything else, my senses as sharp as a recently honed knife. I was aware of the men charging down the hill beside me, aware of the trees and the earth and the sky above, aware of even small details—a broken branch, a mossy stone.

We had almost reached the creek when the Indians opened fire from the opposite side. There are officers who might view such a moment as the perfect opportunity to take cover but Steele wasn't one of them. Brandishing his weapon over his head, he shouted, "Come on, men! Kill all the Indians you can!"

He charged off at full speed and we followed, right on his flanks, those of us in front firing ahead and everyone whooping like the Cree. I saw them, cowed by our numbers and firepower, turn and flee in the direction of the meadow. We were right behind in hot pursuit, splashing through the creek and entering the clearing. I heard the unmistakeable voice of Wandering Spirit ordering his men to form a firing line to stop us and push us back up the hill. I didn't get a chance to explain that to Steele because nobody was listening to their war chief. Some ran for the swamp where others had already taken up position, some went up the hill and still others ran toward the ford. There were bullets zinging everywhere and small explosions of dust erupted at our feet.

Fury and his men rushed the hill as Steele had instructed,

and the rest of us fanned out in the clearing, firing at the flee-ing Indians. A handful of Scouts flushed the men out of the swamp; some of them abandoned their weapons and retreated into the lake while others made for the ford at the narrows. Many were firing at us from across the bay. Amid the chaos I felt a burning sensation on my right cheek as if a red-hot poker had been laid against it, and heard something whiz by. This was followed almost immediately by a thump on my chest, as though someone had punched me hard enough to leave a bruise.

I stopped dead in my tracks and saw a musket ball fall to the ground. I put my hand up to my face and pulled it away with blood on it. Not a lot of blood but enough to show my luck was riding high again, for I had been shot twice. The bullet that had bounced off my chest and fallen harmlessly to the ground must have come from one of the Indians' antiquated weapons, but the one that had creased my cheek was another story. That must have come from a Winchester or a Sharps, as those were the only modern weapons the Cree possessed, and they had precious few of them. Had it been a couple of inches to the left it would have surely killed me. It was a miracle, and if Big Bear had seen it he would surely think I was all but indestructible. And he would probably change my name from Crooked Tooth to Lucky Man.

I saw Steele stop and glance over at me but I started running again to let him know I was all right. My chest was sore and my cheek burned but I was so exhilarated I paid it little mind. Over to my left I could see Fury and his men chasing Indians up the hill. The camp had been cleared except for three wounded men. We took them as prisoners and set the lodges on fire.

The Indians who had crossed the narrows had taken up positions on the treed slope of the peninsula. We found cover on the near-side slope and picked off three or four in the water, until someone shouted, "Hold your fire! There's a woman down there!" I couldn't tell from my vantage point if it was a man or a woman, but the person appeared to be holding a bundle of something. Our guns fell silent but there was still sporadic firing from across the narrows and from over where Fury was.

Shooting resumed as soon as the woman was safely out of sight and continued for a half-hour. Our rifles grew so hot we could barely hold them, but the latter stages of the battle became more a waste of ammunition than a solid offensive. Recognizing the futility of it, Steele had his trumpeter sound a ceasefire. The utter silence seemed preternatural. It hung there for a moment, laced with the smell of gunsmoke, as if neither side knew what it was; then it was filled with the moaning of the wounded.

I was close enough to Steele to see sweat glistening on his forehead beneath his helmet, but with him it was bound to be sweat from exertion and being overdressed on a warm day rather than the heat of the battle. His scarlet tunic still looked surprisingly fresh, all things considered. Using a tree for protection, he stood up, cupped his hands and yelled across the water, a distance of no more than a hundred yards. "You must give yourselves up! Riel and his rebels have all been defeated. We want only your leaders and the murderers. The rest of you can go peaceably on your way."

He turned to me and called, "Tell them that as best you

can in Cree." But before I could utter a word, a reply came in a hail of bullets that splintered the bark on his tree. We resumed firing and the stalemate continued for a few more minutes. Every now and then we caught a glimpse of our quarry retreating north along the far shore of the lake, too distant for a decent shot. Steele ordered an ammunition count. I was down to about a dozen rounds and the others weren't much better off. It was nowhere near enough to warrant a pursuit across the narrows, so we fell back to the clearing.

Bill Fury lay seriously wounded with a bullet in his chest, attended to by the Scouts who had brought him down from the hill. Steele went to him immediately, visibly upset that one of his men was badly hurt. Someone had stuffed the wound with a neckerchief to staunch the flow of blood yet Fury seemed in a positive mood and even managed a smile. He and his men had left seven Indians dead up on the ridge and that eased his pain somewhat.

Steele had a few men convert one of the native wagons into an ambulance, then we all retreated to the big rock and took stock of our situation. Several Scouts had minor wounds, plus me, but Fury was our only major casualty. We estimated the casualties among the Indians to be at least 12 dead and many more injured.

Steele decided that we would dig in and hold this position until General Middleton arrived with reinforcements. He sent a patrol back along the trail to meet him but it returned four hours later to report that the general was nowhere in sight. The news plainly irritated Steele.

"We'll need to go farther back," he said.

"How far back, sir?" asked Sergeant Butlin, the man who had led the patrol to find Middleton and who was reluctant to retreat an inch.

"We're in no shape to fend off an attack, sergeant, so we'll have to go far enough to make any offensive on the enemy's part impractical. Ten miles or so ought to do it. But I want a rear guard here and you're in charge of it. Pick five men and make sure you include Strong. You may need somebody who understands Cree. I wouldn't be surprised if they returned sometime soon to bury their dead, so stay alert. If that's what they're up to, don't pick a fight. Hightail it back to our position."

Steele had the troops leave us part of their remaining ammunition before they pulled out. We were to follow once Middleton arrived to take over.

Butlin, four regular constables and I took up a position in the trees that afforded cover but allowed a view of the clearing and the narrows. We waited for the rest of the day but didn't see any movement, although we heard three shots echoing across the water from somewhere down the bay. The Indians were shooting at something, but it wasn't us and for that we were thankful. Nevertheless, Butlin had us take an occasional pot shot at a tree, just to let them know their pursuers were still around.

That evening, a spectacular sunset reflected off the glassy water of the lake and the lonesome cry of loons amplified a tranquillity and beauty that belied the events of the day. We spent a quiet night. The calm air and resulting silence were our allies as they reduced the possibility of the Indians sneaking up on us. When I bedded down I had to lie either on my back or on my left side because my right cheek was sore where the bullet had opened up the skin. I secretly hoped it would leave a scar, a badge of honour. In my mind I reviewed the charge down the hill and understood that a man would be hard-pressed to make that trip alone, yet with comrades it had seemed an easy thing to do. I felt elated because I had been in the thick of it and had not only survived but hadn't run away. And I knew that in some small way I had redeemed myself for taking flight at Frog Lake.

The following day, as Steele had predicted, the Indians returned to the narrows to bury their dead. They did so furtively, which indicated some concern that we were still in the area and they didn't want to do battle. No one came across the ford to retrieve the bodies that Fury's men had left on the hill. Later, we saw the burial party, apparently finished, moving north along the east shore of the lake, returning to wherever they were camped. Another long night passed and in the morning, we heard riders approaching on the trail behind us.

Advance Scouts galloped up with the news that Steele and Middleton would soon be arriving. We wouldn't be returning to Fort Pitt after all, one said; Steele had managed to per-suade the general that his knowledge of the terrain and his battle-hardened Scouts were indispensable to the mission. This news did not disappoint me in the least. There were still Amelia and her family to worry about and I was keen to get back on Big Bear's trail.

Butlin had other thoughts on his mind. "I hope they're bringing some decent food with them," he muttered.

Middleton and Steele arrived at noon. The general oozed

self-importance but seemed a pompous old fool with his walrus moustache and sizeable paunch, which expanded even as he sat in the saddle. He was sweating and flushed in the warm noonday sun and looked as if he might burst a button on his tunic if he made any sudden movement. Steele appeared to be biting his tongue to keep from saying something he shouldn't.

Despite the intelligence we were able to pass along, that as far as we were concerned the peninsula was deserted, both Steele and Middleton spent several minutes thoroughly scanning the woods through field glasses. When they were satisfied that the Indians had indeed abandoned the area, we mounted up.

We retraced our path from two days before, descending from the ridge and crossing the creek to the meadow. A healthy breeze was blowing and fleecy clouds drifted lazily across the sky. The charred remains of the lodges and spent shells on the ground were the only indication of the battle that had raged there. It had been our crucible of fire, just as Fish Creek and Batoche had been for Middleton's men. Yet I doubt that they considered us equals.

We reached the narrows and crossed to the peninsula. The water was cold and up to the top of our stirruped boots but the footing underneath was firm. On the far side, behind some bushes, we found three hastily dug graves. Concerned that they might hold the bodies of captives, Middleton ordered them dug up. I didn't believe the Indians would have taken the time to bury any white people, especially with us breathing down their necks, and I doubt Steele believed it either. But the general was in charge and he rarely let an opportunity slip by without finding a way to remind everyone of it. It was also plain that he viewed Steele as an upstart and interloper, a mere policeman, not a soldier. Had he seen Steele lead us in that charge through the clearing he would have thought differently.

The men unearthed the bodies and I recognized all of them as Big Bear's warriors. Steele asked if I knew their names and I said no but that none of them were the murderers at Frog Lake.

Steele sent Butlin and me to investigate the area in the bay where we thought the three shots had come from the previous afternoon. We followed the shore along the narrows around a small point of land. In several places snarls of bush pushed out over the water, forcing us inland through the trees. It was hot in that windless environment and the insects were bloodthirsty. We had covered perhaps a half mile when we saw a lodge through the foliage.

We crept closer, silently, hardly breathing, hunched over like old men. We stopped when we had a better view of the lodge and watched and listened for any sign of life. Nothing moved but we could hear a droning sound that seemed to be coming from nearby. Cautiously, we moved forward until we could see all of the small clearing in front of the dwelling. Three bodies lay sprawled by the entrance, bloated, with thousands of flies crawling over and buzzing around them. We waited again, listening for other sounds but heard nothing. Then Butlin said, "It seems safe enough." We unfolded ourselves to our full height and entered the clearing.

The bodies were beginning to smell in the heat and despite

their condition, I recognized them instantly. They were Cut Arm and two of his councillors. All three were lying on their stomachs and each had a bullet hole in the back of his head.

My gut was heaving and not just because of the gruesome scene in front of me. This was murder, plain and simple. These executions were Cut Arm's punishment for freeing me and my fellow prisoners. As to who had done it, I could only speculate—Wandering Spirit, perhaps, or maybe Miserable Man or Little Poplar. All three were capable of such a grievous act. Butlin went back for the officers and while he was gone, I walked away from the bodies. I couldn't handle being left alone with them.

Only Steele returned with Butlin. The terrain was too rough for Middleton's horse and he was too unfit to walk the distance. After thoroughly investigating the scene, Steele sent me for a party to bury the murdered men and destroy the lodge.

North of the narrows, we moved slowly along the eastern lakeshore and found a woman with a rawhide cord around her neck, hanging from a low branch. It appeared as if she had stood beneath the branch, tied one end of the cord to it, looped the other end around her neck, then simply leaned forward. Her lips were an ugly purple and her tongue lolled out of her mouth, black and swollen. There were flies all over her.

"The poor devil," Steele said. "I'll wager her husband is one of the warriors we dug up at the narrows."

We cut her down and buried her.

Farther along the lake, we came to a second narrows, crossed it and set up camp. We found more rifle pits here plus a long marsh that we would have to traverse to continue our pursuit of Big Bear. Middleton tried crossing the swamp and sank so deep he almost didn't get his horse out. He declared it impassable; we would go no farther. Steele was appalled. Had not the Indians passed through it with women and children?

He took it upon himself to find a route and did, his horse never sinking more than a foot or so, but Middleton would not listen. He did not want to have such a formidable obstacle on his rear flank in the event we had to beat a hasty retreat. We would return to Fort Pitt tomorrow at first light.

I could almost read Steele's mind. Beat a hasty retreat from what? A decimated, poorly armed, fleeing band of Indians? Yet it wasn't a lack of courage that caused Middleton to want to halt. He had fought during the Indian Mutiny and was twice recommended for the Victoria Cross. But the job of commanding the Canadian army had merely saved him from forced retirement. He was past 60, badly out of shape for this kind of undertaking and he tired easily, reasons enough for his refusal to go any farther.

Despite Middleton's decision, Steele's curiosity required slaking and he assigned two of his men to investigate the trail beyond the marsh. The task fell to Corporal Willie McMinn and Constable Ralph Bell. I was hoping that Steele would assign me as well but he didn't. However, I wasn't about to let such a minor detail stop me and figured that during the ordered chaos of setting up camp it would go unnoticed if I simply rode off with them. I told McMinn I was coming along whether he liked it or not. He just shrugged and said, "I can't stop you from following me."

Bell was a quiet man with an acerbic tongue when he spoke. McMinn, whose square jaw and face suited the Stetson hat he wore, was just the opposite and would talk your ear off if you let him. He had been with the NWMP since 1881 and claimed he was a "lifer." Luckily, the marsh required his full attention, so he was relatively quiet during the half-hour it took us to cross it. It must have gone on for at least a mile, but both McMinn and Bell were of the opinion that the column could have made it through, even in retreat if necessary.

McMinn said, "Maybe the general wants to go home because he's running low on champagne and caviar."

Bell was even less charitable. He laughed and said, "If there's a bigger jackass anywhere in the Northwest, I'd like know who it is. I've never seen old Smooth Bore bite his tongue so many times."

Old Smooth Bore was the nickname Bell had given Steele, whom he greatly admired.

North of the marsh, the trail split in two, one going east, the other continuing north among the trees. My guess was that the one going east was Big Bear's and that it would turn south for the international border once he was past the lake. The one going north was probably the rest of the Woods Cree. But which group held Amelia and the rest of the prisoners? Or had they been split up too? They had to be alive still, or at least they were up till this point; otherwise, we would have found their bodies. We rode back to camp, which was now nearly invisible in the smoke from the smudge fires lit to keep the mosquitoes and flies at bay. McMinn went to see Steele to inform him of our findings.

Afterward, the corporal sought me out. "Major Steele wants to see you, Strong."

"What about?"

"Well, I've just been dressed down for letting you accompany me so I think you're in for it too."

In his tent, Steele said to me, "I realize your connection to the Scouts is tenuous and temporary, Strong, and I understand that some of Big Bear's prisoners are your friends. But there's a chain of command here that must be observed at all times. You will not go traipsing off into the bush just because it strikes your fancy. Your death in an ambush would have left me with no end of paperwork, and I am a *field* officer, not a desk man. So control your instincts and save me the drudgery of having to explain your demise. Am I making myself clear?"

"Yes, sir."

"You are dismissed, then."

"Thank you, sir," I said. I was halfway out of the tent door when Steele called, "Strong!"

I stopped. "Sir?"

"Bill McLean and his family have been friends of mine for years, so I am just as disappointed as you that the trail ends here. We would be away from here first thing in the morning, covering both trails, were the decision mine. But it's not, so we live with it."

"That's the hard part, sir."

"Indeed it is, lad. Indeed it is."

FOURTEEN

Reunion

IT WAS THE MIDDLE OF JUNE by the time we reached what was left of Fort Pitt. Our clothes were in tatters, we'd all lost weight and if lice were sausages, we could have grown fat on them. Even Steele, usually a model of decorum, looked a little frayed around the edges, his scarlet tunic and breeches in need of a wash and a deft hand with a sewing needle. Of the 68 men and 75 horses that had started out, only 47 men and 25 horses returned. Though Bill Fury and Jumbo Fisk were our only human casualties, and both survived, we'd left the trail to Loon Lake littered with the carcasses of dead animals.

We set up a small city of tents near the ruins of the fort. Steele told me that he would no longer need my services and, after I returned my horse and the government-issued equipment, he saw to it that I was paid from the day McLean had sworn me in, including my time in captivity. The result was much-needed cash in my pocket.

"You're a bit headstrong, lad," he said. "But you have initiative and you're loyal. If you're thinking of a career, you might consider one with the Mounted Police. There's always room for a young man with potential."

"I'll keep that in mind, sir, thank you," I said, and tried to pretend I would give it serious thought. But joining the Mounted Police was the furthest thing from my mind.

Bill Cameron was still not back from the Beaver River and Cold Lake country. According to a courier, they had found Indians but not Big Bear. On June 18, another courier arrived with word that an army patrol near Loon Lake had encountered a group of captives returning to Fort Pitt. They were the last of Big Bear's prisoners and all were well, despite their suffering. Some of the names mentioned in the message were William McLean and his family, and Stanley Simpson.

They came into camp around noon on June 21, in wagons abandoned by the Indians and driven by soldiers. My eyes sought Amelia, and I found her in the lead wagon, which she and her large family filled. She had her arms wrapped protectively around two of her younger siblings and looked exhausted, yet unbeaten. In fact, exhaustion was the common denominator of every face among the hostages, especially the few who were sick with a fever, and Stanley Simpson was the worst of them.

The McLeans were billeted on the steamboat *Marquis*, which was tied up at the riverbank below the camp. I saw Amelia a couple of days later, after she had rested up, bathed and received a change of clothes. She clucked like a mother hen over the wound on my cheek, which had scabbed over. It wasn't more than an inch and a half long and a quarter inch wide and wouldn't have been worth a comment had it been on my arm. But she was aghast when I told her how I acquired it.

"Thank God for small miracles, Jack!"

She wanted to share her experience with me and hear mine, so we found a quiet spot along the river, away from the hustle and bustle of the camp, where the swirling water reflected back darker versions of the bright blue sky and the green bushes lining the bank.

After the battle above Frenchman's Butte, she and the other prisoners and Indians had marched north from dawn till dusk. To save time, they took the most direct route possible, crossing marshes as sticky as gluepots, rather than going around them. Big Bear was intent on putting as much distance between himself and his pursuers as possible. At Loon Lake, he was surprised that we had caught up with them so quickly. They had only just begun to break camp and prepare an ambush when we arrived. (Steele had been right having us hustle to get there, and even more right to descend so quickly from the ridge.) Kitty McLean had injured her knee and had not yet crossed the narrows when we attacked. She had grabbed a child belonging to a Woods Cree family and was wading in waist-high water to the far side when one of our bullets passed a fraction of an inch from her head.

That bit of news sent a chill up my spine. We believed we were avoiding hitting an Indian woman, not one of the McLean girls.

"But why didn't she just stay behind?" I asked. "She would have been rescued!"

"Because the rest of us had already been forced to cross and she worried it might get us killed. Not only that, she was wearing Indian clothes and with her black hair and dirty face she was afraid you'd think she was one of them. The rest of us didn't look any different. No matter, it was brave of her to take the child and cross. Someone not as strong might have stayed, regardless of the consequences."

"Your father and mother must have been in quite a state."

"They were sick with worry but Wandering Spirit would not allow Father to go back to help Kitty. He prayed that she would stay behind because he was confident that the Indians wouldn't take our lives in revenge."

But such optimism was not true of everyone. With the death of Man Who Speaks Another Tongue near Frenchman's Butte and others at Loon Lake, most of the prisoners were afraid that the Indians would take vengeance.

"Stanley Simpson warned us girls," Amelia said, "that not only were Big Bear's warriors going to kill five hostages, they were going to take all of the women as wives too. We knew what that meant and we were worried, regardless of Father's prestige. We didn't know from one minute to the next what to expect."

It turned out that Louison Mongrain, the Woods Cree who had killed Dave Cowan, had taken over as chief since Cut Arm's murder and become their friend and protector. "I think he did it because he felt guilty about killing Corporal

Cowan," she said. "He even gave Father a gun and some shells, and stood guard at night in front of our tent while someone else guarded the back."

The morning after the battle, Big Bear's band pulled out early, heading east to skirt around Loon Lake. After that they planned to turn south and make a run for the border. They had expected Mongrain and the Woods Cree to follow but as soon as the Bear was out of sight, Mongrain moved everyone north. The hostages were excited. They were still prisoners but once they realized that no one was following them, the threat of death didn't appear to be as imminent and there was a feeling that they just might survive their ordeal after all. But that night in camp they received one of the biggest surprises of their lives. Someone had indeed followed them.

Amelia was in her tent when she heard the commotion outside, as if the entire camp had come alive at the same time. She was certain that Big Bear's band had found them and that they were done for. She stuck her head out the door and nearly fainted when she saw Wandering Spirit. But her fears were unfounded. The war chief had come alone. He had sneaked away from his band, seeking refuge among the Woods Cree. He was utterly dejected and his black curls had become streaked with white since the massacre.

When they reached the Beaver River it was swollen with heavy rain and could not be forded. The Indian women built boats out of willow branches and rawhide for the crossing. That night a scout, who had been investigating an area several miles to the northwest, returned to camp and reported that he had seen soldiers. A cloud of despondency hung over the Indians, for they now felt surrounded. They held a council meeting and after a lengthy discussion, decided to release all the prisoners.

The news rejuvenated the hostages. The Indian women made everyone new moccasins, while Mongrain offered a small part of their limited food supplies and a guide to lead them south. Stanley Simpson endeavoured to get even more by helping the band to cross the river. He swam the frigid waters six times and secured extra flour and bacon for them. They lived on that, and the occasional rabbit that Simpson shot, during the few days it took to get back to Loon Lake.

"What we would have done without Mr. Simpson, I don't know," Amelia said. "He is so sick now and although the doctor says it's typhoid, I'm certain it's because he was in the cold water so long."

They were hungry, exhausted and near collapse by the time they reached Loon Lake where, to their absolute delight, they found one of Middleton's oxen, left behind because it had been too weak to follow. They wasted no time in slaughtering the animal, and soon had slabs of meat sizzling over an open fire. At the campsite last inhabited by Middleton and Steele, they found a Winnipeg newspaper that contained the news of Louis Riel's defeat. All were ecstatic, though they still feared an Indian attack and took turns on watch during the night. The next day they encountered Middleton's patrol and their ordeal was over.

"Sometimes I can't tell if this is a dream or reality," she said. "I look at this clean dress I'm wearing and I think it must be on some other girl, not me. And my hands and fingernails are so clean!"

She held out her hands and while they were indeed clean, the skin was rough and, around the nails, raw and shredded. She sighed and looked around. "This moment seemed impossible for so long."

"I know what you mean," I said. I squeezed her hand and she put her other hand on mine. "I suppose you hate Indians now."

"Oh, no, Jack. Not at all! Hate is such an utter waste of time. There's no room in my heart for the ones who did the killings but there's plenty of room for the others. They are absolutely fascinating and I shall write a book about them one day, mark my words."

We sat for a while and didn't say anything, still holding hands. Then Amelia said, "The ship leaves tomorrow at dawn. I think a new posting is in the works for Father. I doubt that I shall ever see you again."

I nodded, not knowing what to say. Yet as we sat there on the riverbank on that glorious summer day, I believed we had formed a bond that would last a lifetime whether we ever saw each other again or not. I felt I could confide in her and admitted just how frightened I had been at Frog Lake and how the guilt still nagged at me for deserting Theresa and Mary, even though they were now safely en route to their homes in the east. I wished that I'd had a chance to talk with them before they left to find out how they felt about it.

"But you would have only gotten yourself killed," Amelia said. "How in heaven's name would that have helped your friends? Think of the burden they would have had to bear if you'd died for them!"

I would try to grasp that perspective for most of my life and still never quite get a grip on it as easily as Amelia did.

I walked her back to the *Marquis* and told her that I would stop by later to wish her family farewell. Before boarding, she said, "In case there isn't an opportunity to say this later, I want you to know how wonderful it's been to know you. I can't tell you how much life at the fort was improved by your presence. I shall not soon forget you."

Before I could respond, she leaned in close and kissed my cheek, then was gone up the gangplank. It was just as well. All the words I knew had once more made themselves unavailable to me.

That evening I returned to the ship to say goodbye to the McLeans. All of them were thinner, but only in body and not in spirit. McLean thanked me for volunteering to join Sam Steele, and I apologized for our turning back at the marsh. "Had it been my decision, sir, I would not have stopped until we found you."

"Of that I am certain," he said. "But things have turned out for the best and that's all that really matters."

He asked me my plans and I told him that my first priority was to return to the coast to see my family. He said, "I would say that the future is yours for the taking and should you ever want to work for the Company, you need only mention my name as a reference. Good luck, Mr. Strong," He shook my hand and before I left to a chorus of goodbyes and thanks from all of the McLeans, Amelia handed me an envelope with my name on it.

"It's a gift to be opened later," she said, a smile lighting her face, her eyes moistening.

Back in my tent, I tore open the envelope, intensely curious about its contents. It was a sheet of foolscap on which was written, "My Dear Jack," followed by the last few lines of Longfellow's *The Bridge:*

> *And forever and forever, as long as the river flows,*
> *As long as the heart has passions, as long as life has woes;*
> *The moon and its broken reflection and its shadows shall appear,*
> *As the symbol of love in heaven, and its wavering image here.*

Beneath, translated into Cree, was the poem in its entirety. Amelia had not been idle during her captivity.

I awoke early the next morning to the whistle of the ship as it pulled out into midstream for its run to Fort Battleford. I hurried out of the tent and saw Amelia standing on the deck. I wondered if she had been waiting for me to appear because she waved straight away. I waved back and watched the paddle wheeler until it disappeared around the first bend, leaving only a pall of smoke over the river.

I barely had time to cobble together some coffee and clear the cobwebs from my brain when Cameron rode into camp, accompanied by General Strange and a small band of Indians. With his arrival I felt that life might at last be returning to normal.

Looking more tired than I'd ever seen him, Cameron told me of his disappointment when a courier brought word of Big Bear's flight to the east. He had hoped to be the one to persuade our friend to give himself up. Not finding Louison Mongrain and the rest of the Woods Cree was salt rubbed into the wound but there was some consolation in the arrest of a handful of Chipewyans who had been involved with the Cree in ransacking Fort Pitt.

"Right now," he said, yawning. "I don't care if I ever see another Indian. Never thought I'd say that but there you have it. I think I need some sleep."

He took his bedroll to my tent and slept the rest of the day and night away.

A few days later, Mongrain and his band arrived at Fort Pitt to surrender. Wandering Spirit was with them.

I knew that things were back to their natural order when Cameron began champing at the bit to get back to work. "There's money to be made here, Jack," he said. "The Indians still have some left, never mind the furs they've got, and all of the troops have their pay. Any man with a lick of business sense would give them a way to spend it!"

"I thought you'd sworn off Indians," I joked.

"One last kick at the can before I quit this country for a while," he said.

"You're leaving?" I asked, taken aback. I had told him many times during our captivity that I was returning to the coast when it was all over but Cameron had never mentioned his intentions.

He nodded. "I need to go back where I came from to collect my thoughts. Think about what I want to do with the rest of my life."

I had assumed that he would stay, because he was as much at home in this land as the Indians, but the events of the past few months had changed the direction of everyone's life.

Cameron had two months' pay from the Company and

with my pay from the Scouts we set out to make some money. We bought two horses and borrowed a wagon and were preparing to leave when Wandering Spirit came out of his lodge and called out to us that if we wanted to see him we should do it now. I believe his exact words were, "All who wish to look at me, come now!" Then he went back inside.

"That doesn't sound promising, Jack," Cameron said, with urgency in his voice. "We'd best get over there."

Others who had understood the war chief's words were also hurrying to his lodge. By then he had already attempted suicide by plunging a knife into his chest. But apparently, he wasn't quite as adept at killing himself as he was at killing others because he missed his heart and survived the wound, although we could see part of his lung protruding from it. An army doctor tucked it back in and stitched him up.

Cameron and I drove to Battleford where we spent all we had on trade goods and new outfits for ourselves. Upon returning to Fort Pitt, we set up our wagon between the soldiers' and the Indians' camps and in three days had sold almost everything. About the only Indian who didn't visit our wagon was Wandering Spirit, although we could see him reclining on a blanket outside his lodge; a canvas canopy had been erected to protect him from the hot July sun.

We went over to see him, more out of curiosity than anything else. He had changed profoundly since I heard him exhorting his fellow warriors at Loon Lake. It was as if his life's blood had drained from his body and left only the husk of the man we had once known. He had metamorphosed from a fierce warrior into a pathetic creature and I could not believe that he was the same person who had once frightened me so badly. When he saw us, a bit of that old fire flared up in his eyes, then died as quickly as it had come. He was too ill and beaten down to sustain any anger he may have been feeling.

Cameron knelt beside him and said, with more sympathy in his voice than I would have been able to muster, "Do you have anything you'd like to trade?"

"No," the war chief said. "I have little. Only 10 cents, if that will buy anything."

Instead of answering, Cameron asked, "What are you eating?"

"Almost nothing. The soldiers bring me flour and bacon but I am not hungry for it."

"Old flour and rancid bacon are no food for a sick man. Where is the knife that you hurt yourself with?"

Wandering Spirit asked his daughter to fetch it for him. She went into the lodge and returned with a formidable dagger, still blood-stained. She handed it to Cameron.

"Let your daughter come with us," he said, "and we will send her back with food that is better for you. In exchange, I will keep this knife to remember you by."

The war chief nodded.

We led his daughter to our wagon and sent her back with a box containing jam, biscuits, canned meat, a bit of butter and some tea and sugar. They were not items for trade; they came from Cameron's personal food supply.

Later, I asked him why he had been so generous with our old enemy.

He shrugged. "I can't say, Jack. He struck a sympathetic

chord in me, I guess. God knows, I don't condone the murders at Frog Lake but maybe he acted in the only way he knew. The view on his side of the matchbox is more cut and dried than it is on ours. Get rid of the white men, and the old ways and the buffalo will return. It was as simple as that to him. And it was there in front of us, as plain as the nose on our face, but we ignored the signs."

"Like Tom Quinn."

"Tom was just the arse end of a much larger mule."

The next morning brought one of those prairie days that you knew would be sweltering by noon and fraught with gigantic thunderclouds by supper time. Colonel William Osborne Smith of the Winnipeg Light Infantry formally accepted the surrender of the Indians and called on them to come forward and lay down their arms. Soldiers in scarlet tunics stood in a line at attention as the warriors walked by and stacked their weapons in a pile. They were then directed to a spot nearby and instructed to sit in a semicircle. When they were assembled, Smith addressed them.

"You are all guilty of taking up arms against the Great Mother. She is, however, a kind woman whose heart is big enough to forgive some of you. Others, though, those who have murdered defenceless white men, must be punished according to the Great Mother's laws. I will call out your names and you will step off to the side."

He read aloud the names from a list that Cameron and I had helped supply. Wandering Spirit, Bad Arrow, Little Bear, Louis Mongrain. Wandering Spirit, brought to the half-circle on a stretcher, was carried to the side. Soldiers chained all of the prisoners like slaves, with the exception of the war chief, and marched them down to the riverbank. There they awaited the arrival of the steamer to take them to Fort Battleford where they would be held for trial. Other soldiers carried Wandering Spirit down. His face was a masterpiece of stoicism.

Smith next called the names of those charged with minor offences, such as theft and destroying property. There were many, perhaps a couple of dozen or more, but they were also chained and marched to the river. Then the colonel spoke to the Indians who remained.

"You who are left are lucky. We know that some of you are just as guilty as those we have arrested. You must never forget the mercy of the Great Mother. Her good grace alone allows you to return to your reserves, where you will be cared for as long as you are good. We will keep these arms that you have laid down, for we can no longer trust you with them. That is all. You may go."

I watched them return to their camp. I had never seen a more dejected group of people. History no longer had a place for them, where they had lived for centuries, and a profound sadness washed over me. What had we done? I would remember this scene as vividly as I would the events at Frog Lake, where I had witnessed the deaths of people. Here, I believed, I was witnessing the death of *a* people. It tore at my heart and I knew what Amelia must have felt, and perhaps Cameron when he gave food to Wandering Spirit. And if I'd had arms long enough to reach out and touch them, I believe I would have done so.

The Indians left for their respective reserves at Onion Lake and Frog Lake at noon. I knew they wouldn't get far that day so, in the freshness of the evening, after the thunderstorms had passed, I said to Cameron, "You know, Bill, I can't speak for you, but I'm up to paying the Indians one last visit. This country's changing so fast I may not get another chance."

"I'll arrange for the horses," he said.

We had sold our horses to another trader but rented them back and rode the few miles out along the Onion Lake road to where the Indians were camped. The rain had dampened the earth just enough to keep the dust down, and the last rays of the western sun turned the summer grass a rich gold. We could smell the smoke of their fires before their lodges appeared beyond a rise.

We were greeted warmly and sat with the councillors around a small fire. The evening had turned fine with a thin wedge of the moon arcing in the sky and a breeze that made the heavens shimmer and kept the mosquitoes grounded. Flying In A Circle, an older, pleasantly disposed councillor who had a reasonable chance of becoming chief, welcomed us to their fire. He lit a pipe and passed it around. While the flames flickered, Cameron and I listened to stories of when times were good and food was plentiful, when men hunted it instead of having it come to them in the form of government handouts.

"We knew ourselves as well as we knew the land for we were one and the same," Flying In A Circle said. "There is so much now that we do not understand."

We slept under the stars that night, side by side with a few of our hosts, and in the morning said farewell as brothers. Cameron and I rode back to the river in silence, an unusual state of affairs for my friend who usually had many paragraphs of things to say.

THAT AFTERNOON, as the thunderheads began building again, word came that Big Bear had been arrested near Fort Carlton, some 140 miles from Loon Lake. Upon reaching a ferry crossing on the North Saskatchewan River, he had stopped at a nearby tent to beg for food. The occupant called for the police, who happened to be just across the river. Arrested with the Bear were one of his sons, Horse Child, and a councillor. The rest of the band had long since deserted him. He was in jail in Prince Albert, awaiting transfer to Regina.

When the next steamer arrived, Cameron left on it for Fort Battleford to see Stanley Simpson who been taken to the hospital there for better treatment. We arranged to meet in Regina for Big Bear's trial where we were to testify on the chief's behalf, after which we would have to attend the trial of Wandering Spirit and several other Indians back in Fort Battleford.

I put to use the carpentry skills Cameron had taught me—he had taught me so much—by hiring on with the Company to resurrect Fort Pitt. Later in the month, news came up from Fort Battleford that Miserable Man had turned himself in. Unconfirmed rumours said that Little Poplar had made it south of the international boundary. So had Little Bad Man.

FIFTEEN

Mercy of the Great Mother

I STAYED AT FORT PITT UNTIL early September, working hard, and the process of building soothed my soul. Gradually, I was able to shift the events of the past few months into a back room of my mind where they were still resident but less bothersome. Yet I had come to realize that what my mother had said was true, that seeing atrocities has to affect a man no matter how tough he thinks he is. For that reason I wasn't looking forward to the trials because I knew they would dredge it all up again, and it was also why I had no desire to ever return to Frog Lake.

The shells of all the buildings had reached completion when I boarded the steamer and went to Fort Battleford. The town hadn't changed much over the past year except that there were many more soldiers around. I bought a horse and a used rifle and, with food that I had scrounged from the Company at Fort Pitt, struck out along the trail to Swift Current where a regular train service connected Calgary with Regina and Winnipeg.

It was less than 200 miles and I covered it in five days, the country being alternately flat and hilly, and all of it sun-burned brown and bone dry. Small, fluffy clouds raced across the big sky in monotonous procession; the days were warm and the nights cool. I passed others along the trail, mainly bull trains, but avoided overnighting with the teamsters. I craved solitude, and made camp well off the trail and out of sight of passers-by.

I hobbled my horse so she wouldn't wander too far and bedded down, trusting that she would let me know if anybody showed up. During the night and early morning, the utter silence of the land was powerful and never failed to fill me with awe. There were great mysteries borne on that enormous silence and I remembered Big Bear telling me during one of our many conversations that his people communed with those mysteries and learned from them. That was why they saw themselves as much a part of the land as a tree or a rock, why all their knowledge was of the land itself. To be separate from it would mean an unbearable loneliness.

REGINA SAT next to Pile of Bones Creek, a damp scar across the face of a dry, bald landscape as flat as a salt pan. The settlement existed because the Canadian Pacific Railway had decided it would and for no other reason. It seemed like a town begging its inhabitants to leave, because every street led to a beckoning, limitless horizon. And like all prairie towns, the harsh winters had taken their toll on the buildings.

I met Cameron at the Queen's Hotel, about which there wasn't the least suggestion of royalty. He had arrived in late July, having, out of plain curiosity, come down early for the trial of Louis Riel. The court had sentenced the rebel leader to hang on September 18, although his lawyers had appealed the decision. Cameron didn't give the appeal much chance of success.

"Oh, they might delay the inevitable, all right," he said. "But he was a dead man as soon as the court opened its doors for the trial. I think that was obvious to everyone, including Riel."

Others that I knew were there for the Bear's trial, among them John Pritchard and Stanley Simpson. Both had rooms at the hotel. William McLean was there, too, without his family, but he was important enough to stay at Government House with Edgar Dewdney, the lieutenant-governor. Amelia had sent her best wishes, he said when I saw him.

Big Bear's trial got under way on September 11, in a temporary courtroom that was crowded and hot. Gaily dressed women in the audience, Mounties in their scarlet tunics and judges and attorneys in black robes contrasted sharply with the chief's ill-fitting and threadbare white-man's clothing. He sat there, stoical, listening to proceedings that he did not understand. He spoke no English and for many phrases, there were no exact Cree equivalents. Just how difficult it was going to be for him was clear from the moment the prosecution read the charges. Altogether, there were four laid against him, ranging from promoting rebellion to sending seditious messages to other insurrectionists. But it was the closing statement, that these offences were "against the peace of our Lady the Queen, her Crown and dignity," that seemed to cause the most confusion.

Big Bear responded through his interpreter. "These people lie. They are saying that I tried to steal the Great Mother's hat. How could I do that? She lives very far across the Great Water, so how could I go there to steal her hat? I don't want her hat and did not know she had one."

There were a few snickers from the gallery. The judge banged his gavel and explained the charges in simpler terms, that "crown" in this case did not mean "hat," but the tone had been set. Big Bear was a foreigner in his own country.

Pritchard, Cameron, McLean and I all testified on his behalf. Cameron said that the chief had been angry when his son, Little Bad Man, along with other band members, had looted the Hudson's Bay store at Frog Lake. He had ordered them not to take anything without asking for it but Little Bad Man, intent on usurping his father's power, had ignored him. Cameron also said that he had heard Big Bear's resonant voice shouting, "Stop! Stop!" when the first shots were fired.

"You did not see him?" asked the prosecutor.

"I did not. But his voice is like no other's."

"Since the accused does not speak English, you must understand Cree."

"Yes, sir. I not only understand it, I speak it."

Cameron went on to testify that, while he was in captivity, he had on more than one occasion heard Big Bear say that the prisoners were not to be killed. The prosecutor asked him to repeat the exact words in Cree, which he did to the complete satisfaction of the court's interpreter.

My testimony was similar to Cameron's because I had only heard, and not seen, Big Bear too, and once my understanding of Cree was established I stepped down. Pritchard said that not only had he heard the Bear but he had seen him running toward the shooting as he exhorted his warriors to stop. McLean attributed the fact that he and his family were still alive to Big Bear's intervention on their behalf. Wandering Spirit and Little Poplar had wanted to kill them and take his daughters as their wives.

Stanley Simpson, to his eternal discredit, would not lend his support. He was angry with the Bear for the ordeal he been put through and blamed him for the illness that had almost ended his life. He testified that he had heard the chief say that he wanted to cut off the prisoners' heads. This brought a gasp from the spectators, which the judge quickly silenced. The defence attorney arose and proceeded to rip Simpson's testimony to shreds, showing the court that he could have heard no such thing. Through a series of questions in Cree from the interpreter, which he failed to understand, the Company man's knowledge of the language was proven to be negligible.

Meanwhile, the Bear sat there, utterly lost for the most part, knowing only that strangers, by some incomprehensible process, were going to decide the course of his life, perhaps even the manner of his death. He was a man who believed in the power of dreams, that they spoke to him and should be heeded. It was fundamental to the Indian way of life and he had often dreamed things that had come true. But never in his worst nightmare had he seen this peculiar room and these alien proceedings that had taken him so completely into their grasp.

Perhaps he had been right when he told me after the sacking of Fort Pitt that the best solution to the Indian-white conflict might be for one side to destroy the other and start all over again. The process, it seemed, was well under way and I wished I could have found a way to shield him from the inevitable heartbreak ahead. But a small avalanche, begun near the top of a legal hill, had gathered substance and speed, and was roaring down upon him, and there was no route to safety. When the attorneys had done their work, the jury took 15 minutes to reach its decision: guilty as charged.

Big Bear's sentencing hearing would take place in two weeks. The jury had asked the court to show mercy but Cameron and I could not stay around to find out just how merciful it would be. Our presence was required back in Fort Battleford for the trials of Wandering Spirit and the others charged in connection with the Frog Lake murders.

ALL TOGETHER, seven Indians had been charged with the killings: Wandering Spirit, Miserable Man, Bad Arrow, Little Bear, Man Who Speaks Another Tongue and two Indians I didn't know but whom Cameron had named: Iron Body and Round The Sky.

Man Who Speaks Another Tongue, of course, was already in a shallow grave north of Frenchman's Butte. Cameron and I testified and they all pleaded guilty, except Miserable Man, which didn't matter. The court deemed him just as guilty as the others. The judge sentenced them all to hang.

Two other Indians, convicted of murders in the Fort Battleford area, also received death sentences.

Dressy Man, convicted of the killing of the *wendigo*, and Louison Mongrain, convicted of murdering Corporal Cowan, had their death sentences reduced to life in prison.

The trial left me at loose ends. I did not think that I was capable of feeling sympathy for people I also considered to be murderers but that's exactly what I felt. I wanted them to pay, but not with their lives. Not even Wandering Spirit.

There were so many prisoners that a special place in the fort's stable had been barricaded off to hold them. But with the death sentences, Wandering Spirit and the other condemned prisoners were moved into smaller cells in the guardroom where a closer watch could be kept on them. Because of our connection to Frog Lake, Cameron and I received permission to visit them the day before their execution. We took tobacco as a gift.

The guardroom contained four large cells in sets of two placed back to back. Access to these was down hallways sealed by heavy metal doors that opened by a lever system. The cells had levered metal doors with small barred windows and everything was whitewashed. Each cell held two prisoners. When one of the guards let Cameron and me into the hallway, accompanied by another guard, and the big door clanged shut behind us, there was a frightening finality to it, like the door of life slamming closed. The guard let us into the cell holding Wandering Spirit and Miserable Man, and shut and locked that door too. He stood outside, waiting and watching.

Both men had heavy chains and balls attached to their ankles. We shook hands and offered the tobacco we had brought. It eased the tension substantially.

Wandering Spirit said, "I am glad you have come, my brothers."

He then spoke of the long road that had led to the events at Frog Lake and how Riel had heavily influenced him four years before, down along the Missouri River. The rebel leader had been trading whisky to the Indians and had complained about how badly the government was treating his people. They were going to demand money and if they didn't get it, they would rise up. If the Indians were to benefit, they should rise up too. The war chief wasn't entirely convinced that Riel was right, until he'd had the dream. He explained it to us.

It had begun with the buffalo, thousands of them, gracing the plains, there to provide sustenance for his people. Snow lay on the ground and in a thicket a recently constructed pound stood ready to receive the animals. Instinctively, he knew where the herd was and rode right to it with another hunter. They circled around behind the animals and stampeded them toward the pound. "*Yei! Yei!*" he yelled to keep them moving. If they changed direction, other hunters jumped up and fired their rifles into the air, shouting "*O-oh-whi!*" and kept them on track to the pound.

"The powdery snow rose like white dust in the sky," Wandering Spirit said, seemingly lost in recalling the dream. "The earth shook as if the Great Spirit himself was angry."

The thundering hooves, even muffled by the snow, made a magnificent sound, "the sound of life for my people."

Once the animals were in the pound, a gate of poles and buffalo hides was pulled shut to enclose them. Suddenly, the hunters disappeared, as did the pound and all the animals except one, a huge bull that stood there snorting and pawing the earth. It was his alone to kill. He raised his antiquated rifle and just as he was about to pull the trigger the animal shifted shapes and became a man. A white man. He could not pull the trigger even though he knew he must. Then a rifle materialized in the white man's hands, so shiny and new that the sun reflecting off it blinded him. And even though he now stood alone, he knew that the weapon was pointed not just at him but at the heart of his people and that there was nothing he could do to stop it. It exploded and woke him up.

"That dream spoke to me of truths," he said. "The buffalo are gone forever and white people cast long shadows across the land, like dark clouds of locusts. The old ways are dying and now my people hunt rabbits and the children are as thin as lodge poles. The white man promises us food but every time we ask, we are refused. That is the way it is with white men. They speak from both sides of their mouths and the truth is whatever suits them."

Following close on the heels of his dream came the lunar eclipse. When he saw a shadow taking a bite out of the full moon, he knew that it would eventually extinguish the moon's light, just as the white man would extinguish the ways of his people. It was a sign only a fool would ignore and it had come at a most appropriate time because he had just received word that the half-breeds had fought the police at Duck Lake and won.

"All these things spoke to me," he said remorsefully. "But I should not have listened to any of them."

He apologized for what had happened and wanted us to tell his daughter that he would die in the white man's religion and that he wanted her and the rest of his family to have that religion too. He had but one request: Could Cameron arrange for him to be shot rather than hanged?

Cameron shook his head, clearly uncomfortable with having to speak of the means of another man's death. "I would if I could but there is nothing I can do. It is beyond my control."

Miserable Man was quiet but when Wandering Spirit finished speaking, that horrid face of his creased with a half smile, the first I'd ever seen on it, and he said, "Tomorrow, my brothers, I go to see my father. That is good. I have not seen him for a long time. I am not yet afraid, but in the morning when the rope is placed around my neck? I cannot say."

Before we left, Wandering Spirit had something to say to his jailers, and asked if we would summon them. Upon their arrival, the war chief stood to his full height and said, "You have been good to me, far better than I deserve. It is a bad thing I have done and my punishment is no worse than I deserve. I had always been at peace with the white man, but I received some bad advice. But it is useless to speak of that now. It is late to say it, but I am sorry. I thank you Red Coats and the sheriff for your kindness. I am not afraid to die."

But he did not want to die with a ball and chain attached

to his leg. When he was told that it would be removed, he said, "Then I will die satisfied! I may not be able to say it in the morning so I say it now—goodbye!"

Cameron acted as interpreter and it was plainly difficult for him. His eyes grew watery as he repeated Wandering Spirit's words in English. I was busy grappling with the thought that two human lives in this cell would no longer exist tomorrow, that while I was going about my daily business they would be dead. The possession of such knowledge was almost overwhelming.

I DID not witness the executions. I could not. I'd seen enough death to last me a lifetime. Instead, I walked out the stockade gate to where there was a lovely view over the North Saskatchewan River valley, pristine white with a thin blanket of snow. I found it preferable to the black view inside the fort. Yet I heard the trapdoors release with a heavy thud, heard the cries of horror from the crowd and heard the Indians among the witnesses begin to wail. I stood there, rooted to the spot, my mind awhirl and unable to focus. I don't know how much time had passed before a wagon trundled out of the gate loaded with eight wooden boxes. It disappeared somewhere down the slope among the barren trees where labourers had already dug a common grave and were waiting to fill it in. I was shaking, from the cold I told myself.

Cameron had stayed until the bitter end, though he had not wanted to. He had been named to the coroner's jury as an official witness, so his presence was mandatory. He told me that he could not rid his mind of the awful clicking sound of eight necks being dislocated. He doubted that he ever would.

Sometime prior to the execution, word came up from Regina that Big Bear had received three years for his role in the rebellion. It was three years too long as far as I was concerned. Upon sentencing, the judge asked if he had anything to say and the old chief had spoken eloquently, not for himself but for his people.

"Your Lordship, I am Big Bear, Chief of the Crees. The Northwest was mine. It belonged to me and to my tribe. For many, many years, I ruled it well. Now I am old and ugly; my heart is on the ground. From now on white men with handsome faces will rule this land. But when the whites were few, I gave them my hand in friendship. No man can ever be witness to any act of violence by Big Bear to any white man. Never did I take the white man's horse. Never did I order any one of my people to one act of violence against the white man. I ask for a pardon and help for my tribe. They are hiding in the hills and trees now, afraid to come to the white man's government. When the cold moon comes the old and feeble ones, who have done no wrong, will perish. Game is scarce. Because I am Big Bear, Chief of the Crees, because I have always been a friend of the white man, because I have always tried to do good for my tribe, I plead with you now; send help and a pardon to my people. Give them help! How! I have spoken!"

Then the Bear took the first train ride of his life, in chains, all the way to Stony Mountain Penitentiary in Manitoba. I don't know how many times I've wondered what that extraordinary old man was feeling as an industrial-age machine bore him to his fate at speeds he could not have dreamed of as a child. I could only speculate, for it was all on the other side of the matchbox and I would never fully know.

I MADE one more trip with Cameron. We travelled south to Swift Current in a caravan of three NWMP sleighs accompanied by officers homeward bound on Christmas leave. In Swift Current, we waited for the trains, one that would take me west and the other that would whisk him away to the east, to visit his family for a while. He was finished as a trader and would be seeking new horizons. We sat up late on our last night together, sipping brandy, much like that night so many months before in Frog Lake, when fate propelled us on a journey I could not have imagined. Cameron spoke of nightmares of Indians hunting him down, after which he invariably awoke in a cold sweat. Yet he bore no grudges because they were not part of his makeup.

"They were afraid," he said. "Afraid of losing the life they'd always known, and fear has caused as much trouble in the world as a need for power. All they were doing was waging war against an invading enemy, and that is no less than what we would have done. Yet the government charged them with treason. The irony of it is heartbreaking."

He was a good man, and I said so as we shook hands at the station, while the inbound train blew its whistle and wheezed up to the platform. I had learned much from him during the year and a half of our acquaintance, more than I could have ever learned in a classroom. He had given me a fresh pair of eyes with which to look at life.

He smiled and said, "Speaking of good men, I happen to be shaking the hand of one."

A good man. I suppose I had grown up some over the past year, at least enough that I didn't feel unworthy of the compliment. "Thanks, Bill," I said and could say no more.

He climbed onto the train, a black iron beast impatient for its plunge over the horizon. All too quickly it pulled away from the station to disappear down the line in a smudge of smoke and steam.

ACROSS THE years, I have often thought of the people I knew, who, like me, were reluctant actors in a real-life play that history remembers as the Riel Rebellion and the Frog Lake Massacre. Cameron, of course, is always foremost in my mind. After he returned home he put his academic education to use and became a pharmacist, although not for long. He eventually married and that didn't last either, for he never seemed able to settle down. He returned to the west because it was in his heart, and moved from town to town, working at whatever he could set his hand to, from farming to government employee to newspaper owner and editor and other jobs in between. His facility with words led naturally to writing and from time to time I would come across his stories of the west in magazines. For a while he was editor of *Field & Stream* and brought the work of the cowboy artist Charles Russell to public attention. But ultimately he was a nomad just like our old friend, Big Bear, and I suppose there is some irony in that too. Four decades passed before I saw him again and that was at

Frog Lake, where we unveiled the cairn commemorating all those who died on that fateful day.

Besides Cameron, I think of Big Bear the most. He haunts my memories. While some of his people lost their lives, he lived to lose a way of life that he revered. The government released him from prison after only a year and a half because his health had deteriorated so badly. It is little wonder. How does a man who has gazed upon limitless horizons for six decades look upon four prison walls? Especially when all he did was stand up for what he believed was right. It surely must have confounded him.

He returned to the Battle River Valley but could scarcely recognize the ragged people living there; they were not the proud race he had once known. He complained that he was broken down and alone. His wife had left him for another man and his eldest son, Little Bad Man, had settled in Montana and had taken most of the rest of the family with him. The Bear contemplated suicide, but ultimately decided that it was a coward's way out. Mercifully, he died in his sleep on January 17, 1888, at the end of a terrible winter storm. His grave is on a low hilltop on Poundmaker's reserve because he never did have one of his own. Perhaps that was his only victory in a war that was lost for his people before it even began.

Poundmaker surrendered to General Middleton at Fort Battleford. He said that he had only wanted food for his people and to live in peace. He was charged with high treason, translated to him as "trying to knock the Queen's hat off with a stick," and sent to Stony Mountain prison. He spent a year there and was released because of illness; he died shortly afterward from tuberculosis, only 44 years old. What, I've often wondered, did he and Big Bear talk about, when or if they had the opportunity? Were their conversations of a philosophical nature? Did they speak of practical things? Were their words fiery with anger? Tinged with sorrow? Or were they rendered speechless by the strange stone walls confining them?

Little Poplar made it safely to the United States but died before Big Bear. A half-breed shot him one night during a drunken fight.

I never saw Amelia again, nor any other member of her remarkable family. Her mother and father and siblings all survived their ordeal without a shred of bitterness. Furthermore, Mrs. McLean had been pregnant at the time. She and her husband ultimately expanded their brood to a baker's dozen. As for Amelia, she went with them to Prince Albert after their captivity, then to Fort Alexander on the shores of Lake Winnipeg where her father had accepted another posting with the Hudson's Bay Company. He eventually took them to Winnipeg where he retired and she became a translator for Indian Affairs. I had carelessly lost her poem not long after we parted but many years later, I was pursuing one of my favourite pastimes of browsing through a bookstore when I saw a slender volume entitled *People of the Plains*. It was a sympathetic treatise on the Plains Cree and its author was Amelia McLean Paget. I purchased a copy, hurried home and devoured it in a single sitting. It was clear that she had attempted the difficult journey to the other side of the matchbox and that she saw what was there better than most.

Of the NWMP officers whose acquaintance I made, I don't

know what happened to Loasby other than that he managed to survive his wound. But Frank Dickens retired a few months after the rebellion and embarked on a speaking tour of the United States, hoping to reap rewards similar to his father's. Few of his life's endeavours had ever met with much success, however, and this would turn out to be his biggest failure: he died of a stroke in Minnesota before reaching his first speaker's podium. As for Sam Steele, he was a man who would stride through history and carry many, including me, in his wake.

I HAD time to spare in Swift Current until the westbound train arrived, and some money too, so I bought myself a pair of warm woollen socks, a shirt, a buckskin coat, a high-crowned Stetson hat and western boots. The boots were going to take some getting used to but I felt like a new man as I walked to the station in a light snowfall, and boarded the train with an enthusiasm borne of new beginnings. Calgary, not Granville, was my destination because, despite a recent gathering of dignitaries in the mountains of British Columbia to complete the railway east to west, regular runs wouldn't start until the following summer. I'd have to spend another long winter and spring east of the Rockies before I could get home to see how Ma was doing.

As the train lurched forward, a thin, bespectacled man dressed in a fine overcoat and derby hat placed a leather valise in the overhead rack and took a seat opposite me. He smelled of whisky and tobacco.

"Whew!" he said, breathing hard. "I almost didn't make it. Going to Calgary?"

I nodded.

He offered his hand with a smile. "Ed Hayes. The I.G. Baker Company. Sales. It would appear that we are stuck with each other for the duration of the ride."

I would rather have had the seats to myself but he seemed a decent sort. I shook his hand. "Jack Strong," I said.

"Yes," he said, sizing me up. "You could be."

As things worked out, I was grateful to have met Ed because he was instrumental in getting me hired at the I.G. Baker Company, unloading freight and working in the store occasionally. It was heavy work but it got me through the long Calgary winter in relative comfort and with a full belly. I was at the front of the line when tickets for the first scheduled train to the coast went on sale.

Author's Note

THERE IS MUCH HISTORY IN THIS story but first and foremost it is a story, meant to entertain rather than instruct. However, if it inspires the reader to delve deeper into this fascinating episode in Canada's history then a secondary purpose will have been fulfilled. With that in mind, I have included a suggested reading list at the end.

For those interested enough to visit the "massacre" and battle sites, there is a large cairn just east of the present village of Frog Lake that commemorates the event and those who died there. Seven of the victims are buried near the cairn along with Dave Cowan, the North-West Mounted Police corporal killed near Fort Pitt. A few interpretive cairns line one edge of the site and several yards away, across a dirt road, the foundation of the Catholic church can still be seen.

There is also a cairn at the site of the Battle of Frenchman Butte (called "Frenchman's Butte" at the time), which actually took place about three miles north of the butte itself.

The rifle pits dug by the Indians and the hostages are still identifiable.

An interpretive cairn sits on the hill occupied by the Scouts and overlooks Steele Narrows, where the Loon Lake skirmish took place, although the narrows has been filled in and a road crosses it. White crosses mark the spots where some of the Natives fell but these places were not easy to get to when I visited there.

Little remains of Fort Pitt except one old building that was erected after the fire. The ridge that played such a prominent role during those violent times is still there, of course, but is now a farmer's field. The North Saskatchewan River still flows placidly by.

Fort Battleford, on the other hand, is a developed tourist site with guides dressed in period costumes and is well worth a visit. The old jail that held Wandering Spirit and Miserable Man is still standing and is accessible for tourists. For fans of Charles Dickens, a complete set of his works—first editions— presented to the fort by Frank Dickens, sits on a wall shelf in one of the buildings. As one would expect, they cannot be handled.

Acknowledgments

I wish to thank Peter Thompson for planting the seed for this story; Philip Teece for the maps and his encouragement; my editor, Marlyn Horsdal, for her perseverance and faith, and all the folks at TouchWood Editions for their diligent work. As always, special thanks go to Jaye. Without her unflagging support, neither this nor any of my other books would exist.

Suggestions for Further Reading

Ahenakew, Edward. *Voices of the Plains Cree*, McClelland & Stewart, Toronto, 1973.

Beal, Bob, and Macleod, Rod. *Prairie Fire: The 1885 Northwest Rebellion*, Hurtig Publishers, Edmonton, 1984.

Brown, Wayne. *Steele's Scouts: Samuel Benfield Steele and the Northwest Rebellion*, Heritage House Publishing Company, Surrey, BC, 2001.

Cameron, William Bleasdell. *Blood Red the Sun*, Hurtig Publishers, Edmonton, 1977.

Charette, Guillaume. *Vanishing Spaces: Memoirs of Louis Goulet*, Translation by Ray Ellenwood, D.W. Friesen and Sons, Altona, Manitoba, 1976.

Dempsey, Hugh. *Big Bear: The End of Freedom*, Douglas & McIntyre, Vancouver, 1984.

Hughes, Stuart, Editor. *The Frog Lake Massacre*, McClelland & Stewart, Toronto, 1976.

MacGregor, J. G. *Edmonton: A History*, Hurtig Publishers, Edmonton, 1967.

Stewart, Robert. *Sam Steele: Lion of the Frontier*, Doubleday Canada, Toronto, 1979.